THE PUPPET

Modern Middle East Literatures in Translation Series

THE PUPPET

A NOVEL

IBRAHIM AL-KONI

Translated and Introduced by
WILLIAM M. HUTCHINS

The Center for Middle Eastern Studies
The University of Texas at Austin

Cover art: *Tele*, by Hawad. By permission of the artist.
Cover and text design: Kristi Shuey
Series editor: Wendy E. Moore

Library of Congress Control Number: 2010928912
ISBN: 978-0-292-72335-1

Originally published in Arabic as *al-Dumya* (Beirut:
al-Mu'assasa al-'Arabiya li-l-Dirasat wa-l-Nashr, 1998).

CONTENTS

CHARACTERS

Abanaban, chief vassal

Aghulli, sage and leader

Ahallum, warrior hero

Amasis the Younger, a noble

Asen'fru, tax administrator

Chief Merchant, the man with two veils

Emmamma, venerable elder

Imaswan Wandarran, spokesman for the council of nobles

She-Jinni, the Mute Soprano

Tayetti, commander of anti-gold campaign

Wretch, a young lover

INTRODUCTION

> My starting point is the desert. As is inevitable with
> one's birthplace, the desert buries enigmatic signs
> in the souls of its natives that slumber deep within
> and one day must awake. The signs that my Great
> Desert planted within me have made a poet of me,
> and a seeker after the truth of this world.[1]

Ibrahim al-Koni, who was born in 1948, is an international
author with many authentic, salient identities. He is an award-
winning Arabic-language novelist who has already published
more than seventy volumes, a Moscow-educated visionary who
sees an inevitable interface between myth and contemporary life,
an environmentalist, a writer who depicts desert life with great
accuracy and emotional depth while adding layers of mythical and
literary references the way a painter might apply luminous washes
to a canvas, a Tuareg, whose mother tongue is Tamasheq, and a
resident of Switzerland since 1993. Ibrahim al-Koni, winner of the
2005 Mohamed Zafzaf Award for the Arabic Novel and the 2008
Sheikh Zayed Award for Literature, has also received a Libyan state
prize for literature and art, prizes in Switzerland, including the
literary prize of the canton of Bern, and a prize from the Franco-
Arab Friendship Committee in 2002 for *L'Oasis cachée*.

After spending his childhood in the desert, al-Koni began his
career writing for the Libyan newspapers *Fazzan* and *al-Thawra*. He
then studied comparative literature at the Maxim Gorky Literature

---

1. Ibrahim al-Koni from an interview conducted by his friend and German
translator Hartmut Fähndrich, as translated from German into English by
Rafaël Newman. Posted online at: http://www.swissworld.org/en/switzerland/
resources/why_switzerland/ibrahim_al_koni/.

Institute in Moscow, where he also worked as a journalist. He later lived in Warsaw for nine years and edited the Polish-language periodical *as-Sadaqa*, which published translations of short stories from Arabic, including some of his own. His novels *The Bleeding of the Stone*, *Anubis*, *Gold Dust*, and *The Seven Veils of Seth* have already been published in English translation, and *The Animists* is forthcoming. At least seven of his titles have appeared in French, and at least ten exist in German translation. Representative works by al-Koni are available in approximately thirty-five languages, including Japanese.

Ibrahim al-Koni, like Joseph Conrad, has found international acclaim as a novelist while publishing primarily in his second language, in his case Arabic, which he learned to read and write at the age of twelve. Al-Koni grew up speaking Tamasheq, the language of the Tuareg, which has its own alphabet, Tifinagh, that dates back at least to the third century BCE. Arabic-Tamasheq bilingualism among the Tuareg is not uncommon and evidence of this goes back hundreds of years in the form of inscriptions and graffiti in Mali.[2]

The Tuareg, or Kel Tamasheq, are traditionally pastoralist, nomadic Berber people who have moved freely across the Sahara from Libya, Tunisia, and Algeria to Mauritania, Mali, Niger, and Burkina Faso. Today national boundaries and policies hinder this migratory pattern, and during the last fifty years there have been armed Tuareg insurrections in Mali and Niger.

Although the Tuareg have been affiliated with Islam for centuries, a tribal code of law still governs traditional Tuareg life, despite the fact that its written version is no longer extant. Al-Koni consistently refers to this Torah-like law with the word *naamuus* to distinguish the Tuareg law from Islamic Shari'a law. Although there are some excellent studies of the Tuareg (like *The Lesser Gods*

---

2. See: P. F. de Moraes Farias, *Arabic Medieval Inscriptions from the Republic of Mali: Epigraphy, Chronicles, and Songhay-Tuareg History* (Oxford & New York: Oxford University Press, 2003, for the British Academy) p. cxxvii.

of the Sahara by Jeremy Keenan), al-Koni's own publications remain the richest source for information about Tuareg culture.[3]

Tuareg culture has attracted considerable attention from outsiders. The blue veils worn by Tuareg men have fascinated intrepid travelers and ethnographers for decades.[4] More recently, Tuareg musical groups like Tinariwen and Tartit have achieved international renown, and the Tuareg Festival in the Desert (in Mali) draws visitors from around the world. Tuareg jewelry is sold commercially through the Internet and elsewhere. Furthermore, the Tuareg poet, painter, and calligrapher Hawad, who provided the cover art for this volume, can be seen reciting his Tamasheq poetry on the Internet site YouTube.

Ibn Khaldun (1332–1406), the Arab father of sociology, described the rise and fall of Middle Eastern dynasties, which he said spring from hardy desert nomads (like the Tuareg). When they are united by *'asabiya*, or group solidarity, they are able to conquer the reigning dynasty in the capital, but after several generations of enervating city life and several stages of governmental consolidation and withering, this now decadent elite falls to the next group of hardy desert nomads united by some new form of group solidarity.[5] *The Puppet* [*al-Dumya*] (1998) is the central and key panel of a triptych—composed of *Waw al-Sughra* [New Waw] (1997) and *al-Fazza'a* [The Scarecrow] (1998)—that traces the Khaldunian development and eventual decline of an oasis named in honor of the Tuareg's "lost" oasis, the paradise-like

---

3. Jeremy Keenan, *The Lesser Gods of the Sahara* (London & Portland: Frank Cass, 2004) with a bibliography pp. 266–273.
4. Covering the head and face has clear utilitarian advantages in a dusty desert, but Tuareg male veiling also has a mystique that is often discussed with awe by al-Koni's characters. See: Chapter 3 (The Judgment), part 2 of *The Puppet*.
5. See: Ibn Khaldun, *The Muqaddimah: An Introduction to History*, trans. Franz Rosenthal (Princeton: Princeton University Press, 1958) vol. 1, pp. 353–355, for example, but *'asabiya* is also discussed in later volumes of *Kitab al-'Ibar*. The simplified version of his theory here leaves out details that do not apply to *The Puppet*.

Waw, pronounced like the English word "wow." Even now this "distant oasis lying beyond every other oasis" occasionally appears, but only to searchers who are not looking for it.

The Puppet focuses on the cusp of the Khaldunian cycle when commerce, marriage, agriculture, and recreation—whether games or cultural activities—are oasis distractions that disrupt the traditional Tuareg nomadic way of life. Consequently *The Puppet*'s hero, Aghulli, who still respects Tuareg nomadism, is devastated to learn that his secret supporter is exactly the wrong sort of (mercantile) person.

The Puppet is a completely realized tragedy at both personal and communal levels. If the flawed hero Aghulli experiences the reversal, recognition, and suffering of an Aristotelian tragic hero,[6] the oasis community's flowering inevitably leads to its withering and eventual destruction. Plato in *The Republic* discussed the different types of states, which correspond to types of people, and their degeneration. Al-Koni in *The Puppet* captures the moments in this arc when the withering sets in as an aristocracy (rule by the best: the venerable elder Emmamma) degenerates first into a timocracy (rule by the ambitious: Aghulli, the sage, who succumbs to ambition) and then into an oligarchy (rule by the rich: the chief merchant). Plato's character Socrates remarked: "The downfall of timocracy is due to the flow of gold into those private stores we spoke of."[7] Aghulli's campaign against gold makes perfect sense in this framework.

Although the novel's title brings to mind contemporary allegations of political manipulation, the author has stressed repeatedly that he is not a political writer. According to him, *The Puppet* portrays a good man who has been asked to lead a

---

6. See: Aristotle, *Poetics* (3.4.3) 52b10.
7. Plato, *The Republic of Plato*, trans. Francis MacDonald Cornford (New York & London: Oxford University Press, England 1941, American Edition 1945, 17th printing, 1960) p. 274, Chapter XXX(VIII.550).

corrupt society. Al-Koni's political fiction is philosophical, and some readers have complained that these novels are intellectually demanding. His elegant, formal Arabic can also be challenging and suggests a clear and simple but formal English rendition, with an occasional modern word added to rouse the reader from any mythical slumber. Regardless of its philosophical potential and language, *The Puppet* is most of all a gripping, expertly crafted story of bloody betrayal inspired by both gold lust and an ancient love affair.

The title character of *The Puppet*'s sequel *al-Fazza'a*—the scarecrow—already appears as an enigmatic jinni in *The Puppet* and then becomes a key player in the oasis community's death in the final book in the trilogy. In *The Puppet*, this visitor from the Spirit World, despite an occasional muffled snicker, appears to try to help Aghulli, the noble if obtuse leader. Al-Koni's satanic figures—like this scarecrow or like Seth in *The Seven Veils of Seth*—often resemble the Yoruba god Eshu, whose tricks and mischief provide spiritual guidance by giving people a jolt. Al-Koni's "good demons" shock other characters, as in *The Seven Veils of Seth*, into resuming the questing, yearning life of the nomadic pastoralist, thus adding an extra fillip to the rags-to-riches cycle described by Ibn Khaldun: the return of a corrupt elite to a healthier nomadic life.

In Islamic West Africa, where societies retained elements—like masquerades—of their pre-Islamic culture for extended periods and where Sufism has been an important strand in the Islamic tapestry, spirituality is multifaceted and it is not surprising to see this diversity reflected in al-Koni's fiction. The ancient goddess Tanit, whom the Tuareg worshipped before the introduction of Islam, figures in some novels, and inhabitants of the Spirit World, many of whom are jinn, maintain an uneasy truce with their Tuareg neighbors. Typically, al-Koni's heroes feel a special bond with their ancient Saharan ancestors and the rock inscriptions they left behind. In novels like *Anubis* and *The Seven Veils of Seth*, al-Koni added ancient Egyptian ingredients to his hearty spiritual stew. In *The Puppet* the subplot about the young lovers continues a Sufi theme of the possible transformation of carnal into spiritual (mystical) love.

Al-Koni has written dozens of desert novels, some set in a mythic past before the arrival of Islam, others in the medieval Islamic age, and still others in contemporary times. For al-Koni, the tension between nomadism and settled life is not only found among Saharan peoples but affects all of us as we face hard choices like relocation for career advancement. If scientists model human medical conditions on laboratory creatures and other inquirers use one phenomenon as a metaphor for another, al-Koni might be said to model global issues on Saharan life. Al-Koni has often used the same Saharan model, but he has employed it as a metaphor for a wide spectrum of human concerns.

> My desert is the metaphorical desert, the desert as synonym for the entirety of human existence. By which I mean that human existence is in every particular a desert as long as it remains a meaningless talisman. But on the day upon which this secular world takes on significance, on the day upon which the world bears down to tell us of its truth—on that day, and not before, shall we witness the separation of the world from the world-as-desert. And on that day, and not before, will I allow myself to rest from speaking about the desert in its function as symbol of existential alienation, what is known in religious discourse as 'sin'. That is why it is obscurantist to see any connection between writing about the desert and living in the desert.[8]

---

8. http://www.swissworld.org/en/switzerland/resources/why_switzerland/ibrahim_al_koni/.

THE PUPPET

In its requisite rational form, profit-oriented (economic) existence, when actualized to furnish each worldly culture with material goods, is essentially devoid of love. Every variety of activity in the rule-governed world is encumbered by this same defect.

Max Weber, "Theory of the Religious Directions of Rejection of the World," from "Zwischenbetrachtung," 1915

The blood of the world's most sacred and robust possession has been shed by the blows of our knives. Who will wash the blood from our hands?

Friedrich Nietzsche, no. 125, *Die Fröhliche Wissenschaft*, 1882

The Ruler wished to abdicate in favor of Immodest Daring, who refused. The Ruler offered his throne to Tzu Chou the Stalwart, who said, "Do you want me to become the Son of Heaven? I think that is conceivable, but I've contracted a disease. Invalids must devote themselves to searching for a cure and should not become involved in arranging matters they don't have time for. Even though world sovereignty is important, I don't intend to destroy myself by assuming power."

◉

The Ruler offered his throne to the Sage of Solicitude, who responded, "I stand at the heart of space, in the heart of time. I wear skins in winter and cover my body with clothes woven from grasses in the summer. In spring I plow the earth and plant, exercising my body. In the fall I harvest my crops and rest my body after its exertions. Sunrise always brings work and sunset always offers repose. Between the heavens and the earth I find delight in my heart and in my reasoning self-contentment. So what would I do with world sovereignty? Oh, you don't understand my true nature!"

After he refused to take control of the world, he left immediately. He ventured far into the mountains—no one has ever found where.

Then the Sovereign offered the throne to his friend Farmer, Master of the Stone Gates. Farmer replied, "I feel unequal to the task, because I would be responsible for violent men. I cannot compete with my sovereign's qualities."

Then he glanced at his possessions and placed bundles on his back. Taking his wife and children by the hand, he set off toward the sea and did not return. No one ever saw him again.

○

After that the Sovereign offered the throne to his northern friend He-Who-Does-Not-Know-Choice. He replied, "You, master, are eccentric! You once lived a humble life in the fields and now loiter in the sovereign's palace. You're not satisfied with that but wish to defile me with your filthy deeds. You don't know how ashamed I feel for you."

Then he went and threw himself in the Ching Ling's watery depths.

○

A final man to whom the world's throne was offered responded, "You, my sovereign, asked for my advice when you planned the attack against Cleave-In-Two, wishing me to appear in the guise of a rebel. After your conquest over Cleave-In-Two, you come to me, offering to abdicate control over the world in order to satisfy a longing to make me appear greedy. It's true that I was born in times of insurrection, but I cannot allow a man who lacks the Tao to defile me with his filthy deeds twice over."

Then the Conscript threw himself into the river Chou's waters and drowned.

The Ruler had recourse to the Sage of Dark Light, meaning to abdicate. . . . The latter said, "Seizing power is wrong. Killing one's subjects is a desecration of the law of compassion. Committing a crime for personal gain makes one an ignoble person. I've heard that it's inappropriate to enter the land of a man who lacks the Tao. So how can I allow others to honor me? Oh, I can't take any more."

Then the Sage of Dark Light rose and, strapping a rock to his body, threw himself into the river Lu.

Chuang Tzu, "Abdication," *The Book of Chuang Tzu,* fourth century BCE

THE SHE-JINNI

1

Since its founding, the oasis has received many people, and clans from the desert's four corners have settled there. Its walls have sheltered unknown wayfarers—most of them men but a few women as well. Some were excellent folks and others vile ne'er-do-wells. Among them were well-adjusted individuals; others conducted themselves in an eccentric way, exhibiting aberrant behavior.

It is said that this difference in qualities and defects of natures was typical not only of the men of these nomadic races but also of some of the women. Informed sources agree that Waw never experienced a creature more seditious or one who aroused greater agitation and curiosity than the lone female traveler whom narrators called the Mute Soprano.

Local history buffs say she arrived from the south and entered Waw at twilight, through the Oases Gate. Her timing fed the conviction that this visitor had no ties of kinship with the desert's people and was instead a she-jinni and the daughter of the Spirit World, because the tribe normally considered guests arriving at twilight to be jinn cloaked in human garb. The inhabitants of the oasis had inherited from their forefathers beliefs affirming that every creature that stirs at those frightening moments just before sunset is kin to the Spirit World's inhabitants.

She appeared alone, and no woman had ever arrived in the settlements of the oasis in this way before. By coming alone, she lent credence to the assertion, based on the soundest authority, that she was related to the noblest jinn. Unlike all the foreign women who had journeyed there before her, she was not accompanied by a spouse or relatives or attended by slaves or female servants.

She arrived on the back of a fearsome, short, well-nourished, large-mouthed, thick-haired camel with a crazed look in its eyes. Children joked about its appearance and repeated in unison that it was a jinni's steed bearing the daughter of the jinn. On the behemoth's back was fastened a howdah that astonished everyone who saw it. The frame was composed of polished ribs bound together. Experts affirmed that these were cut from the tusks of an elephant slain by an ignoble hand. Woven around the arches of these curved beams were animal skins. Coverings of colorful, pure linen, which was decorated with embroidery of tiny beads of many hues, were braided around sheaths. Small white beads adorned the dark linen hangings and red ones embellished braided strips brightened by light colors. Thus the whole construction had been transformed into an extraordinarily beautiful masterpiece around which children hovered while the women gathered to inspect it. The men's eyes were refreshed as they admired and contemplated it, trading compliments for it. They eventually agreed that the ensemble was a verse of poetry and not a howdah at all.

Skeptics were quick to find in the howdah's beauty new evidence for their claim about the visitor's lineage. On peering beneath the saddle to scrutinize this marvel, they discovered that the howdah was attached to the body of the fearsome behemoth by leather belts that had dried into its skin after encircling the belly, thus making it impossible to remove the howdah, which had adhered to the camel's back, becoming one with its flesh, as if it were an extension of the hump on which it sat. The behemoth puffed out its jowls and cast furious glances from its angry eyes at the curiosity seekers, as if it were a hostile jinni. Then it went off to graze in the woods of the southern sector, without the howdah ever leaving its hump.

2

They scrutinized her figure the moment she dismounted. She had a heavenly build, a firm body, and a relatively slender torso. Her complexion was pure, untouched by the darkness of the southern tribes, and the features of her face had a sweet charm. She had bright red cheeks, and a mysterious, delicate smile glittered in her green eyes. She was clad in a flowing blue gown, and the inhabitants of the oasis immediately noticed her silence.

They stepped forward to meet her and caused her frightening camel to kneel. They showered her with the sweet compliments customarily reserved for nobles and leaders, but she did not respond to their greeting with even a word. Instead she granted the throngs surrounding her an enigmatic glance. She smiled at the children in a sibylline way desert people find only among the female jinn.

She did not favor them with this smile for long.

The stern look they had noticed when she arrived returned to her enchanting green eyes along with the sad expression so typical of wanderers and foreigners. Her pupils retained the hint of her smile, but the gleam was extinguished as a painful reserve settled over her eyes, which lost none of their beauty as a result of this change. In fact, their seductive look was reinforced. Mystery flashed from them, their enchantment increased, and beauty's tyranny became more complete.

At this moment, people heard that voice.

It was a voice never before heard in the desert.

People were at a loss when they tried to think of a comparable sound. It was likened to the rustling of a calm breeze through retem boughs. It was said to be a strange, muffled wail. Others declared that it resembled more closely the groan of misfortunes.

The painful moan began as faintly as the distant drone of a fly. Then it drew nearer and grew louder and mightier until it filled every ear. People's breasts were convulsed by worries they had never before experienced. Mystics were inflamed by the sweetest forms of longing, and tears flooded all eyes. The oasis shook, cavaliers reeled, and hearts felt drained. Some became so intoxicated that they fell from the roofs of their homes. In musically induced ecstasy, men and women began writhing in ditches. Some were so overcome by grief that they drew their swords and stabbed themselves. Another group lost their minds; they sang a little and then went insane.

The melodies of the beautiful woman, who communicated only through song, were lethal.

3

They embraced the she-jinni.

They erected tents for her out in the open and slaughtered animals for feasts. The women of the tribes gathered around her, and at evening parties female poets sang for her the refrains of eternally lost souls. Old women kept her company at celebrations of the full moon. She would furtively cast a grateful look at people and then gaze off into a maze of emptiness while summoning to her chest the lethal voice that would almost have destroyed the tribe's mounted warriors had the temple's woman diviner not directed the tribe's nobles to use drums to drown out the melody. A troupe of young women cradling wooden drums with skin heads surrounded the foreigner's daughter, who paid no attention to the commotion till the girls' fingers began to beat the drums so loudly that the plaza resounded. Then the pounding drums cut short the tongues' clamor and swallowed the breasts' growls.

The planets, however, went down different alleys, and the stars swiftly changed places and entered ill-omened houses. The diviners' blind eyes saw Saturn slip over to dwell in Pisces's tower and Venus leave her territories to station herself in Scorpio's home. So the open spaces were flooded with the cunning of the celestial bodies, and iniquity lodged in the oasis's settlements. Then people were awakened by a wail that rocked their buildings' pillars and hearts were penetrated by a desolation they had never known before. Once more male poets began to stab themselves and female poets threw themselves off the tops of walls. This occurred because the foreigners' daughter had been insulted; the horizons resounded with this calamity's wail.

4

During the first days it was said that—thrilled by the she-jinni's beauty—a stranger, whom the oasis had recently welcomed, had sought her out late one dark night, hoping to be alone with her. Later, however, sages acquitted the sons of foreigners of this deed, saying that eyewitnesses had seen a scion of the nobles shoot past in the gloom, fleeing after calling for relief from his calamities.

Shortly thereafter, lips whispered to each other that more than one man had intruded on the beauty's tent, that one love-struck man had slipped in beside the girl in her bedchamber before the other and had begun to pour into her ear the type of lie that the tribe's cavaliers customarily poured into the ear of any object of their affection, because they felt certain that lying is love's talisman and that passion is a treasure attainable only by prevarication. The foreigner's daughter, however, was rankled by this intrusion and jumped up in alarm. Then the second suitor arrived and lay down in another corner of her bedchamber. When the new arrival discovered the presence of a rival, he attacked. They exchanged insults and drew their swords. The she-jinni's terror increased and she found herself obliged to avail herself of her fatal voice. So she sang her moaning lament.

The identities of the two rivals might have remained a secret forever had people not noticed that the two most prominent nobles in the oasis were confined to their residences. Thus Aghulli missed the council, and the hero Ahallum did not attend either. So the sages sent someone in search of them, but they both sent their apologies, alleging an unforeseen illness. When the council's members visited in order to reassure themselves, they found that Aghulli had fastened an imposing bandage around his left wrist and that the hero had wrapped his neck with thick cloths, which he attempted to conceal beneath his veil. The matter might have remained merely conjectures concocted by the imaginations of the populace, who were unable to enjoy life without novel rumors and imagination's embellishments, had the nobles of the oasis not noticed the frigidity between the two rivals, who had recently been close friends. They now avoided each other. When they did meet and were obliged by the laws of the council to converse, they spoke with an antipathy not lost on discerning individuals. Earnest folk (who always spoke wisely in the tribes' settlements although no one paid any attention to them) said, "When strife flares between two friends, we don't need to search for some distant secret, because a beautiful woman, like a serpent that bites and immediately spews out its venom, will be positioned nearby."

5

Confusion prevailed and wails resounded within the walls of the oasis.

Women howled behind the mute sibyl, and girls and boys cried aloud. The most intellectually resolute participated too by lamenting and weeping for a long time.

Despite the enormous uproar, the she-jinni's voice soared above the houses with the wings of a bird, descended from the heavens like a revelation, and swallowed the crowd's voices. It overcame the disorder and was clearly audible, pure, comprehensible, and painful, invoking some undisclosed calamity, presaging seduction, death, and a quest for a distant objective.

In every corner and space people rubbed shoulders, and folks congregated in the temple plaza. The streets were packed, and citizens flooded down the alleyways till the market was jammed. They spread through every open space as far as the bare ground by the well and the heights of the fields adjoining the Oases Gate.

The council convened, and the hostile glances that the two rivals exchanged while they continually wiped away tears did not escape clever people, who were sobbing too. The most steadfast men in the council were content to hold back their tears and sob privately. They carried in the venerable elder on a litter woven from fronds and leafless palm branches. One of the slaves stepped forward and picked up the frail body, which he deposited at the center of the council as if it were a heap of straw. Emmamma immediately sat up and straightened his elegant veil, which was dyed a gleaming blue. After glancing at everyone with his small eyes, he proceeded to stare off into space before swaying and releasing the lengthy moan that could only have emerged from the chest of a creature who had craved the life of eternity and had long been liberated from his painful existence among men. This sigh of other homelands was a balm for those suffering from the thrusts of the jinn's songs. Later the nobles claimed that Emmamma had demonstrated greater fortitude than they not because of any mysterious power but because old age had deafened and protected him against the tune that poisoned the bodies of the impudent and flattened the strongest men of the tribe. Others went further, saying that the secret lay in the origin of his moan; Emmamma won because he had procured his song from the land where the mute woman had obtained her lethal tune.

On that day, Emmamma spoke with a tongue the heavens plucked from each of the elders, because those who possessed a tongue were resisting the affliction and had lost their minds. He terminated a debate for which people had no strength by saying, "Raise the matter of the woman intruder with the temple's virgin. Or, have you forgotten that we only resort to that place to appeal for someone to speak to us intelligently when afflictions have deprived us of the intellect's grace?"

Everyone groaned tearfully, and the council's messenger advanced, weeping, toward Emmamma.

6

That day Imaswan Wandarran performed a feat recounted for generations and celebrated by female poets in their songs.

They said he had been monitoring the situation from the start, searching for a stratagem that would allow him to counter the threat. So he hastened to a trencher and made dough from flour while trembling with dread, desire, and longing like all the other warriors. Then he stopped up his ears with bits of this dough. Thus the sound and his fever were diminished. The voice did not vanish forever, but he chanted ballads to overpower the song of seduction and to slay the melody. He carried the bowl to the alleys, where people were swarming and wails and roars resounded. He hastened to the warriors and began to shove dough in their ears to restore them to their senses. He found the herald shouting and calling for the nobles to convene a council. So he thrust dough in his ears and rushed forward to rescue as many as he could. He collected a group of warriors and forced his way through the crazed throngs, proceeding till he reached the weeping soprano's tent. He assaulted the mute woman and gagged her mouth with a piece of linen. Then people attacked him, but the warriors defended him against the mob and expelled the she-jinni from the settlements of the oasis. People threw stones at him, spat after him, brandished swords, staffs, and knives in his face, but he was able to take the female intruder far away.

The messenger returned with the female diviner's admonition. With tears in his eyes, he read the piece of leather: "The leader sends you the good news that the civil disturbance has been buried, the danger has ceased, and the tribe is no longer in need of counsel." The nobles did not understand this report until they learned what Imaswan Wandarran had accomplished. Listening carefully, they discovered that the voice hovering over their heads had fallen silent.

7

Informed sources related that eventually people of every age and race trailed after the woman, following her down ravines and over the elevated ridges to the north. Once the burden was removed, the affliction dispersed, and people awoke from their intoxication. Survivors then followed the trail, searching for their kith and kin, but found that everyone who had accompanied the accursed woman had died of thirst and disorientation. As for the she-jinni, they never found any trace of her.

THE PUPPET

1

In the blacksmiths' market, he gestured to Aghulli that he wanted a word with him in private.

They silently traversed the alleys leading to the temple plaza, where they saw a throng of nobles standing in a circle and debating with a wariness born of respect for ceremony. The two men avoided the group and went off to the east. They walked along in silence until they reached the secluded area leading to the fields that lay beyond the spring.

There the hero spoke for the first time, "I wanted to share with you what the commoners are saying."

Aghulli smiled enigmatically and rolled a smooth stone with his elegant sandal. He perused the tracks on the patch of earth: human tracks and those of animals as well. Camels' hoofprints were superimposed on human footprints, and human feet had trampled camels' hoofprints. Reptiles crawling through the nights' gloom had attempted to erase the tracks of both people and beasts. Mice had come to swipe grains of barley from the camels' droppings, and dung beetles had rolled dung to their lairs.

The smile in Aghulli's eyes grew more enigmatic. The hero Ahallum spoke. "They came to me yesterday for the third time, repeating what they told me the first time."

He stopped. Aghulli did not respond, and so the hero paused a moment before saying, "They said they want to have a leader, like all the other tribes."

He fell silent. Aghulli also clung to the stillness, and their footsteps sounded twice as loud. Their breathing resembled the

Qibli's roar.[1] They covered some more distance and entered the thicket of date palms adjoining the spring's boundaries. Then Aghulli spoke for the first time, "Aren't they content with the tomb's leadership?"

"They said they want a leader who walks on two feet."

"Have they observed in leaders who walk on two feet any wisdom greater than that of our leader who rests in the temple's tomb?"

"Who can convince the populace? What tongue can debate with the masses? In the past I thought that heroism was demonstrated by the sword's blade. But in recent years I have started to question this conviction. I have begun to see that true heroism is not achieved by the sword. Persuading the gullible to proceed down the path of wisdom is an incomparably greater form of heroism."

"How determined do they sound?"

"They not only sound determined but act obstinate."

"I don't like this!"

"If you want me to be candid, I'll tell you that I not only found their conduct to be obstinate but detected in their language the whiff of a conspiracy."

"Conspiracy?"

"Yes. They debate with merchants, experts, and strangers by night and then pound on the doors of noblemen by day, making heretical suggestions."

"You're right. Abandoning the leader's way seems ill-omened."

"Worst of all, people won't continue on the path declared by prophecy much longer."

---

1. The Qibli is the south wind, from the desert.

"You're right. In this campaign is concealed a conspiracy that seeks to lead members of the tribe from the true path and send them back to the land of earthly rulers who walk on two feet."

"For this reason I wanted to consult you before expressing an opinion in the council of nobles."

"You've done well, because they wouldn't have come to you had they not given up on me."

The hero stopped and gazed at his companion with genuine astonishment. He was silent for a time. Finally he cried out, "Really?"

Aghulli bowed his head. He perused the secret signs in the tracks of the mice, dung beetles, and lizards. Then he said, "They spoke for a long time and numbed my head with arguments they had dredged up somewhere. They said that people who spring from the earth need an earthly leader, while people of the heavens need a heavenly one. They said that the Law will never pardon the council the error it committed in choosing a creature who had become a heavenly person and appointing him commander over the earth's communities. They said that the sons of the heavens were created to assume responsibility for those in the heavens, not for those who struggle on their feet in the desert's desolation. They said . . . they said a lot and favored me with arguments I almost believed."

"Really?"

"I don't know whether jurists would term these whispered insinuations, but to tell the truth, I found a disorienting temptation in their arguments, even though I wouldn't say they're right."

"Really?"

"But tell me how you answered them."

The hero sighed deeply, the way exhausted and miserable people do. He clasped his hands behind his back, studied the horizon, which was flooded with copious late-morning sunshine, and then said, "What could a man whose profession has been learning how to grasp a sword—not dwelling on matters that require the intellect's judgment—say? Yes, I told them each time that leadership has never been the responsibility of heroes. I told them that they ought to call on me during a raid and not approach my house during peacetime. I told them that my place is beside the leader, not on the leader's throne. I told them that they would need to search for a leader among those who have learned to use their heads, not from men who only know how to use their hands."

"You did well."

"I don't know whether I did well, because I detected nothing in their conduct to indicate that they were convinced."

"It's impossible for the tongue to convince a man who has decided to achieve his goal at any price."

"You're right. And what I realized was that they weren't thinking with their minds but with their hearts."

They walked through the Oases Gate. Beyond the wall of the oasis extended a level, barren wasteland that was constantly reborn and crossed by wayfarers gripped by a feverish longing for its eternal horizon.

Aghulli said, "What perplexes me is the use they make of tribal histories when setting their hearts on acquiring a leader who walks on two feet."

"I'm afraid they've derived no benefit from these and are guided by desire, which led earlier generations of commoners."

"Did you say 'desire'? I won't conceal from you my fear of this word . . . for some secret reason I don't understand."

"You're right to fear desire. I heard a sage say that we will never fear the almighty Spirit World if we don't fear desires."

"Are we obliged to surrender to the desire of a people who have adopted desires as their law?"

"We have no choice."

"Why are we obliged to submit?"

"Because we in the council of nobles are a minority and they in the oasis are the swarming majority."

"In the wasteland, even though they were the swarming majority there too, the council never yielded to their desires."

"The wasteland has a law and the oasis another. In the wasteland there is the desert, which is the finest coach for the desires of passionate people."

"I never thought of that before. It seems the desert is truly sovereign over the hearts of the masses."

"Don't imagine that people obey a ruler merely because he's wise. The desert, however, is a priestess on whom the leader depends more than on the prophecies of the diviner, the opinions of the nobles, or even the dicta of the ancestors."

"I've really begun to share your point of view. In the past, power's secret lay in the desert's hand."

"Today, though, power is in their hands, not the desert's, because the walls of the oases nourish in people's souls a ghoul that dozed when we lived in the desert."

"Why didn't I ever think of that before?"

"This ghoul is what we metaphorically and cryptically term 'desire.'"

"Bravo! Bravo! I didn't realize till today that you're a sage."

"My longtime companion, don't try to beguile me with this praise, because when I dismissed them yesterday I told them to return to you today."

"What are you saying?"

"I'm saying I told them they should fix on you, if the intention to select a leader from earthly folk overwhelms them, because you're mentally the most suitable nobleman. Since my only skill is swordplay, choosing me for this august post might lead to an error it would be impossible to correct. That's because they might find their heads falling to the ground during an angry outburst of the type generations have witnessed from heroes since antiquity. Hee, hee, hee. . . ."

The hero continued to cackle, and so Aghulli laughed along with him for a time. Then he stopped to ask in astonishment, "Are you serious about what you said?"

"Completely serious. I told them I would harvest their heads with my sword. So they got scared. Hee, hee. . . ."

"Did you really advise them to return to my house?"

"When you go home, you'll find them at the door. I'll bet a milch camel that they have increased in number and will shortly rush toward your house. Hee, hee. . . ."

He tightened his veil around his cheeks and lifted it to cover his nose. Then he said, "But let's stop kidding around; I've never seen a nobleman more suited for succeeding the leader than you."

"You shouldn't give me so much credit!"

"Why shouldn't I think well of you?"

Aghulli was silent for a time. He gazed at the horizon, which was washed with the forenoon's rays. Then he asked morosely, "Have you forgotten the embarrassing episode with the she-jinni?"

The hero smiled. He rolled a stone with his sandal. He also fled to the eternal horizon. Then he said, "There's nothing at all shameful about noblemen slipping into the bedchambers of beautiful women. We inherited this practice from our forefathers. Have you forgotten?"

"I haven't forgotten, but fighting over a beautiful woman is shameful."

"Here you're mistaken. Warriors and noblemen only fight on account of beautiful women. Do you want them to fight—like the hoi polloi, of whom we were just speaking—to acquire possessions?"

"But our peers censured us in the council at that time."

"They censured us with their tongues, but in their hearts they wished they had been us."

"I've heard people define shame as one friend raising his sword against another on account of an itinerant soprano."

"Don't listen to everything that's said. The only legitimate reason for a friend to raise his sword against his mate is a dispute over a belle. Haven't you heard the panegyric poems written in our honor by young women?"

"What the women poets referred to as an exploit was called by wise men a reckless deed inappropriate for two pillars of the council of noblemen."

"But I'm a warrior, and a warrior can't live without passion, even if all the sages of the desert agree it was a reckless deed. Ha, ha. . . ."

"And what about a person who has never considered himself a warrior?"

"The whole tribe considers you a warrior, not merely because you confront enemies with a sword, but because of your splendor, which you didn't inherit from an ancestor and didn't receive from those before you, since it's a gift that can't be given. People call it nobility, and what is chivalry if not nobility?"

"You want me to forgive myself for that tomfoolery."

"You know I've never said anything I don't truly believe."

"I know, but you exaggerate my good qualities."

"Let's set that aside and return to the question of leadership. Don't forget that a crowd is waiting for you at the door of your house."

"What do you want me to tell them when I find them there? Didn't I tell you I've repeatedly dismissed them?"

"I fear you won't be able to dismiss them this time."

"What are you saying?"

"What's fated is inevitable."

"What do you mean?"

"That for you to yield to the public's will is a thousand times better than for the people to have recourse to some adventurer and impose him on us as a sultan whose pawns we will become."

"What moves you to this foul suspicion?"

"The law of the oases drives me to even fouler suspicions."

"The law of the oases?"

"Yes. We shouldn't forget that the desert hasn't followed us to the oasis and trailed after us inside the walls. We've lost our ancient brace and must adopt the language of the oases and adhere to their laws, if we desire the life here."

"I've actually never thought of that before!"

"The walls serve as a brace for commoners, but nobles will never be safe."

"Amazing!"

"Walls are always the commoner's homeland."

"Amazing!"

"In the desert, tribes need wisdom to live. To live in an oasis, tribes need a stratagem."

When his companion did not respond, he continued, "Indulgence toward the rabble is the first, secret clause in a stratagem's protocol."

"Indulgence?"

"Call it indulgence, leniency, or conciliation. Choose whatever name you like. But the obstinacy you detected in their behavior is what inspired me to think of a strategy that avoids riling or angering them."

"Have things reached the point that we're afraid of these people?"

"Here you forget that we're now citizens of Waw and not residents of the desert. Here you're forgetting that the throng knocking on the door of your house is the stronger power bloc, because the walls support them against us, granting them power seized from us. So beware!"

"I'm amazed by your words."

The hero remained silent, and Aghulli repeated, "I'm amazed by your words."

2

Ahallum spoke to him about splendor.

Ahallum said that he was a warrior too, because he cradled in his breast a gift he had not inherited from any forefather nor received from any predecessor.

Ahallum also said it was a gift that could not be bestowed and called it nobility. Did he believe this? If he did, was it possible for a man, in whose breast traits of nobility lingered, to plunge into the ocean of commoners, adjudicating their quarrels, settling disputes among merchants, laying down rules to restrain thieves, hooligans, and adventurers?

He acknowledged now that the insinuating whispers had grown louder whenever he had reflected on sovereign power. Even if he had not seen in the slumbering leader a model that joined nobility and wise governance, doubts would have multiplied inside him, and he would have known for certain that it was impossible to unite the splendor the hero referred to as nobility and the gravitas manifested by the minority—dubbed the elite—who received from the Spirit World power to take charge of people's affairs.

The day's discussion with the hero had revived his doubts about governance and awakened once more insinuating whispers, by distinguishing between the inhabitant of the oasis and that of the wasteland. Yes, yes, he had said that man in the oasis was formed of a different clay and unrelated to man as known to the desert tribe. Did he believe that? Did man change from one night to the next? Could man exchange his heart the way a snake sheds its skin? Could inanimate walls raised with rows of mute stones borrow the sovereignty of the Spirit World's denizens and fashion from desert man another type of person—as the hero had suggested? How could piles of inert matter abrogate the Law and substitute another law for it merely by being lifted from the ground and placed in walls, roofs, and barricades? How could the desert act as a weapon in the hands of a desert tribe's leader while walls became a weapon for inhabitants of oases to use against the rule of the oases' leaders? Would it not be stupid for a person to renounce his peace of mind in order to take charge of the affairs of a community that owed its nameless authority to nameless stone?

He descended into Retem Valley, where he walked a long distance along the valley bottom. In the retem shrubs, a bird warbled a song, an ancient, touching melody that the tribes commonly scrutinized for omens, because this species of bird was heard but not seen. If one ever happened to show itself, the observer became incorporeal too, because he would not be able to accompany the bird to its realm in the Spirit World without losing his body in the human realm.

As he wandered, he listened carefully to the nameless song. The melody echoed in his ears for a long distance, until he had passed the Oases Gate and made the circuit of the empty area that bounded the wall on the southwest, in order to enter the oasis by the Western Hamada Gate. The singing continued to reverberate in his ears, reminding him at times of the leader. The bird's mysterious melody did not fade until he traversed the alley to find a throng of commoners at the door to his house.

3

The council convened in the temple.

The men sat in a circle in the oblation chamber on mats woven from *diss*.[2] Slaves carried in the venerable elder on a palm-branch

---

2. *Ampelodesma tenax*, a low-growing grass.

litter and placed him at the front of the council after setting around him leather pillows decorated with designs and talismanic drawings. Propped up in this way, he looked even punier and more emaciated. Imaswan Wandarran leaned toward him and shouted in his ear, "Has this heresy reached our master's ears? Have they told you they intend to replace the leader from eternity with a puppet selected from earthly people?"

Emmamma swayed from side to side. His beady eyes, which had lost the brilliance that had long glowed in them, hung in the void. He mumbled the obscure cry that in recent years had become his mantra. It was a melodious chant reminiscent of a song of longing: "Hi-y-y-yeh."

The hero entered, decked out in blue robes. His waist was encircled by an expensive leather belt meticulously decorated and ornamented with small beads. At his left side hung an impressive scabbard, which was also covered with ridges of rich embellishment. In this lengthy scabbard was thrust his mighty sword, although its hilt, which was wrapped with strips of colored leather, jutted up haughtily. In his right hand rested an even more majestic weapon: a spear decorated with fascinating dangling leather straps that flowed down from the upper part of the shaft and quivered with a lovely tremor each time the spear's blade struck the earth as it kept time to the steps of the warrior, who used his fearsome weapon as a walking stick in peaceful times.

He stood at the entrance and cast an all-encompassing look at the council. He spoke as if intending to stifle the song of longing in the venerable elder's chest. "It would be best if you began. There's a crowd following me. They're swarming outside. If you don't expedite matters, I can't guarantee that they won't storm the council."

Amasis the Younger shouted censoriously, "Storm the council?"

The hero squatted beside Aghulli and asked, "What's to prevent them? Haven't you noticed that times have changed?"

"How have times changed?"

"Times have changed because the location has changed. The desert has a law but settlements have another."

"I don't know what the hero's talking about."

"We ought to start at once."

Amasis the Younger straightened his veil and fastened the top over his nose. Turning toward the hero, he said, "The fact is, we didn't wait on you. We began a little while ago. Imaswan said they intend to replace eternity's leader with a puppet chosen from the earthly folk."

Ahallum replied at once, "A change of place brings a change in the times. Only the wasteland's people need the voice of the Spirit World, which you refer to as eternity. Worldly people want nothing from their world but worldly puppets."

Silence reigned. The nobles exchanged stealthy glances, as they normally did whenever they disapproved of something, were biding their time, or were preparing to pounce on a proposal they opposed.

Imaswan Wandarran interjected, "Does the hero mean what he says or have I misunderstood him?"

Ahallum responded with the frigidity that tribes encounter only from true heroes whose exploits are transmitted by successive generations. "No, my stalwart comrade has understood correctly."

"Do you think we should abandon the path of the one who— while he reposes—has left us this land and surrender control to a creature like one of us?"

"If you hadn't acknowledged that we possess land, there would have remained at least one argument in your quiver; or, was your acknowledgment a slip of the tongue?"

"Does the possession of land change anything?"

"Yes, it does, comrade. Possession is also a choice. Didn't the wasteland's law teach us that a person who possesses land is possessed by his land? Didn't our forefathers advise us to beware of remaining in one location for more than forty nights? The ancients included this among their precepts because they understood land's secret nature, because they perceived that the wasteland's law differs from that of the oasis."

Outside, voices grew louder, but Imaswan Wandarran waved his hand in the air as if shooing away flies. Then he said emotionally, "Does the hero think we ought to agree to pick a leader from among us to humor the mob assembled outside this sanctuary?"

"What's fated is inevitable."

"Doesn't the hero know that relinquishing our leader actually means relinquishing the prophecy?"

"What's fated is inevitable."

"Why do you think this is inevitable?"

"Because I know that settled people will never be satisfied with a prophetic leader. They have a greater need for a puppet chosen from the people of this world."

"What are you saying?"

"They claim they want a leader they can see with their own eyes and touch with their hands, someone who will walk among them on two feet, who will resolve their disputes, supervise their affairs, make decrees to benefit them, and set penalties for fraud, burglary, plunder, and acts of vandalism. They say they want a leader, not merely because they need someone to whom they can submit their concerns, but because they can't feel secure and sleep won't find a path to their eyes unless they know that a creature of this kind exists somewhere inside the walls of this oasis."

Imaswan looked at him in astonishment, and the members of the council gazed at him with even greater surprise. Meanwhile, Aghulli was smiling secretly and enigmatically while his fingers fiddled with the *diss* mat. Finally, Imaswan spoke. "You should have attempted to sway them rather than deliver their heresy to our ears."

"My comrade can try to sway them, because they've come to tell you today exactly what they told me yesterday."

Silence reigned over the oblation chamber. Outside, the people's clamor grew louder. Imaswan asked, "Do you really want me to go out to them?"

"If you don't, we'll be forced to choose someone who will act for you and all the rest of us."

"I've never been good at public speaking."

"You've never been at a loss for an argument. You've never lacked eloquence."

"But, my voice. . . ."

"We'll call the herald. I've sent someone to search for him."

"I see you've thought of everything."

"I consider this the lesser evil than civil strife consuming the oasis."

"Civil strife?"

"It would be wrong to underestimate the common people. It's said they're like children before a sage and like an inferno before a fool."

The seated man pressed the *diss* mat with his palms to control his emotions and cast a sweeping glance round the council as if asking for help from its members. The hero gestured to him encouragingly, but Imaswan Wandarran looked off in another direction and addressed the venerable elder with words that blended earnestness and jest. "Have you heard, master? They're set on replacing eternity's leader with the fool's leader. Does our master find any point to their bickering?"

The venerable elder's eyes narrowed till the whites were no longer visible. He swayed like someone overcome by a catastrophe. He keened his everlasting lament, "Hi-y-y-yeh!"

At the chamber door, a powerful man wearing a black turban peered in. The sleeves of his gray tunic were hiked to his shoulders, revealing arms that were also gray and were sculpted with bulging muscles that twisted like the roots of some trees. He crossed his arms at his waist prior to announcing: "The herald awaits permission to enter."

4

In the circular plaza that surrounded the sanctuary on all four sides, citizens crowded together. Even though the area appeared packed, the adjoining alleys continued to spew forth new folks who had banded together in small knots or encountered each other as individuals on the streets. They bumped turbans at times to whisper to each other about the conduct of the conspirators and then shrank back to argue loudly with one another.

Even though their voices created a fearsome growl unprecedented in the oasis, the voices in the area near the eastern walls of the temple were more daring than all the others and became a veritable, detestable cacophony.

The sun was heading toward its zenith.

The members of the council left the chamber and lined up parallel to the wall, with Imaswan Wandarran at the center. To his left stood Aghulli. The hero stationed himself on his right, thrusting his mythic spear into the earth beside him. He had drawn his sword, about which female poets had recited so many poems that people deemed it a legendary artifact from the ancients' myths.

The slaves bearing the palm-branch litter appeared, and Aghulli stepped to the left to make room beside Imaswan Wandarran for the venerable elder.

A sudden silence seized the plaza.

The silence evolved into a stillness the tribe had only experienced in the desert.

It was a stillness people had forgotten since they erected buildings, settled inside houses and walls, and surrounded those walls with barricades and fences, welcoming within these redoubts caravans, foreigners, and wayfarers.

They enjoyed the silence and delighted in listening to the stillness, hearing spiritual songs that are audible only when the world is still. The silence, however, terrifies people who have never known solitude and never savored the taste of stillness in the desert. The quiet frightened the crowds, because from eternity it has been hostile to anyone who has lost his psychological bearings. Man flees to seek refuge among crowds, because he cannot bear the stillness. He could not bear the stillness now either. So he fidgeted, whispered, and muttered.

The mumbling grew louder. Then the venerable elder responded with his refrain, which he had borrowed from the dictionary of eternity, "Hi-y-y-yeh."

Imaswan considered this cry a good omen and seized the opportunity to speak, "I have heard . . . the council has heard that the inhabitants of the oasis intend to reject the oasis's master who rests in the tomb to replace him with a wretched puppet chosen from earthly people's puppets."

The herald sprang into the gap between the crowd of people and the row of noblemen. He called out in a resonant voice that seemed to outstrip his compact body: "I have heard . . . the council has heard that the inhabitants of the oasis intend to reject the oasis's master who rests in the tomb to replace him with a wretched puppet chosen from earthly people's puppets."

A row erupted in the throngs. Angry and disgusted shouts rang out. People at the rear brazenly brandished fists threateningly in the air.

Somewhere in the front lines a voice was raised, "They call the earthly leader a puppet. We call the comatose leader a corpse."

Other voices repeated this statement as if seconding the appeal and making fun of the herald, who had repeated the nobleman's words. "They call the earthly leader a puppet. We call the comatose leader a corpse."

The noblemen's scion tightened the veil around his face and pulled it higher till it covered his nose. He lowered the upper portion until it shielded his eyes. The other noblemen perceived that he was hiding his perplexity, since they knew that this glorious scarf was designed to ward off anguish and to succor veiled nations during confrontations. The scion of the nobles was still for a longer time than protocol allowed. So the hero secretly nudged him with his elbow.

Without uncovering his face or eyes, Imaswan asked, "Don't you know that renouncing the leader's Law entails renunciation of the prophecy?"

The herald leapt forward once more and, clapping his hands over his ears, chanted this query so melodiously that his performance stirred their admiration.

Then silence dominated the area.

The stillness did not last long.

Soon the same voice burst forth again from somewhere in the front row, "Let the dead supervise the affairs of the dead. Bring us a leader from among you."

The throngs snatched up this phase and repeated the call, roaring in unison. The appeal was reiterated with spontaneous emotion even though it seemed once more an ignoble jest intended to poke fun at the herald's craft.

Imaswan shouted desperately, "If you've decided to renounce the Law today, don't blame us if the heavens renounce you tomorrow."

The herald clapped his hands over his ears again, directed his head toward the sun, tensed his muscles like a rooster, and repeated the speech, as if it were a beautiful chant full of poetry's sweetness and a song's melancholy.

At that moment, a wiry man sprang from the swarms in the front line. Wearing a striped djellaba, the man had wrapped the veil around his head in a ludicrous fashion. A piece of faded linen concealed the top part of his head, and another piece of the same color was wrapped around his lips, cheeks, and chin, without covering his protruding ears. This individual was not merely wiry, he was also short. When he spoke, the whole crowd recognized his voice as the one that had been challenging the nobles' scion throughout the debate. He seemed to be addressing the herald and not the council of nobles, who were lined up against the wall. "You should understand that we have demonstrated a lot of confidence in you by asking you to choose a leader for us from among yourselves."

The masses trumpeted this thought and some voices repeated it numerous times, accentuating the provocation.

The nobles' scion asked with astonishment, "What do you expect us to say, immigrant?"

The herald leapt forward like a grasshopper, stopped his ears with his palms, and once more tensed his body like a cock before he seized this phrase from his master's mouth and cast it to the heavens.

Silence reigned for a brief moment. Then the man with the wiry figure rushed forward until he almost rammed the herald with the tip of his turban. He shouted loudly, "I meant to say that these folks could just as easily select a leader from among themselves . . . someone just as wise as any leader with a lengthy tribal pedigree. But because we think well of the sage standing beside you, we have come to present ourselves to the council."

The crowd attempted to repeat this new charm, but the imperfections of their voices turned the refrain into a detestable din.

The scion of the noblemen asked in a critical tone, "What do I hear? Have you gone behind our backs and chosen a leader from among us?"

The herald captured this phrase and leapt into the air like a grasshopper in the fields. He clapped his hands over his ears before casting these words melodiously into space.

"We have chosen Aghulli, master. We have chosen Aghulli with the unanimous agreement of the intellectuals."

"You have designated intellectuals among yourselves too?"

The herald prepared to spring into action but the nobleman stopped him with a stern gesture of his hand.

The short man replied, "The truth is that we've been intellectuals for a long time—wise men from day one."

"Wretch, to what day do you refer?"

"I'm speaking, master, of the first day, our birthday."

"Amazing!"

"It's never good to insult another person."

"Are you a merchant or a transient?"

"I'm neither a merchant nor a transient."

"Are you from one of the tribes of vassals?"

"Vassals?"

"The symbol on your head attests to your status as an immigrant or the son of vassals."

"Symbol?"

"The turban. Only an immigrant or a vassal would tie a veil in this fashion."

"Does our master see some relationship between turbans and leadership?"

The mob grew restless. Then, feeling emboldened, they laughed openly, loudly, offensively. Their laughter revealed a spirit of derision and Schadenfreude.

THE JUDGMENT

1

He set off for a walk through the barren lands.

He emerged from the alleys on the south side of the oasis, crossed the area reserved for caravans, reached the well, and leaned over the stone wall encircling its opening. He was diverted by the trickle of water that continued to flow down a damp ditch with weeds on both sides. He tarried by the irrigation ditch, enjoying the water's sound as it prattled and raved in its struggle with the ditch's rock. The watercourse zigzagged east and then turned west before disappearing in thickets of date palms, grapevines, and pomegranates. In a patch of ground between the trees, at the center of a field to the west, the plentiful waters glistened—seditious and naughty in the twilight. He remembered how the tribe had struggled to find this treasure's location and recalled in detail the day that the beneficent herald had made the rounds repeating the good news. He felt downhearted, however, when he pictured himself clasping in his arms the old well-digger—the earth's victim—to raise him from the belly of the earth. He had known that the tribe would lose the well-digger. The tribe had also realized beforehand what the well-digger's fate would be. The well-digger, who was fond of tunnels and who had learned the earth's secret once he had chosen it for his eternal refuge, himself understood that the day he struck water would be his doomsday. The tribe would not have known he knew had he not confided the matter to his son, who circled the encampment, weeping, before earth's offspring decided to enter the earth to struggle and search for the treasure.

He would never forget the day he descended to the bottom to pull the man out. He would not forget the enigmatic, mocking look that had settled in the well-digger's eyes. He would never forget his tunic, which was soiled with blood and dirt moistened by the spring's water. He would never forget another matter that he had kept from everyone and that remained his breast's secret even now. When he had removed the piles of gravel, mud, and rock and had felt the victim's pulse, he had been certain the man was dead. Then, when he had strapped the body to himself—so that the two bodies (the live one and the dead one) cohered into a single creature thanks to the palm-fiber rope—and when he had tugged at the rope to signal to the men to begin hauling them up, at that moment, he had felt warmth course through his partner's body and had felt with his chest, which was strapped to the victim's breast, his partner's heartbeat. That had not been a fantasy, because the necessary pulse continued during the trip from the pit's bottom to the mouth of the well. He had also clearly felt his partner's heart stop once light flooded over them and the men's hands grabbed them. It had happened shortly before the men untied the fiber rope from their two bodies. He had sensed the mysterious rhythm recede and weaken before vanishing. As it disappeared, the warmth in his partner's body diminished. Their two bodies separated and a fever convulsed him. A fiery tear sprang from his eye and in his heart he felt a thorn's prick. Then he withdrew at once, fleeing from the group's din to bury his pain in the wasteland.

2

On the ridge overlooking Retem Valley, a ghostly figure appeared, emerging suddenly from the retem thickets. He walked alongside the other man at a nobleman's pace, his hands clasped behind him. As if to himself, he said, "It's not a good idea for a person who has assumed responsibility for a people to walk alone, defenseless."

His voice was husky, a scarcely audible whisper. Although erect, he was leaning forward. Like a wayfarer long separated from other people, he searched the stone monoliths, which were flooded by twilight's rays, for a nameless sign. Recluses do not look their companions in the eye and pay no heed to their associates. They shoot past people without noticing their existence. They are, however, a breed fascinated with observing the bodies that unite again at the eternal horizon, even though the tribes perceive these to be inanimate objects or the wasteland's emptiness. Recluses hunt for a prophecy in wayside objects and spy on the Spirit World's inhabitants, who do not show themselves to other human beings. Perhaps for these reasons, the desert's tribes are accustomed to regarding members of this enigmatic community as creatures who always provoke debate, doubts, and suspicions.

Watching with curiosity, he asked, "Is my wasteland companion a stranger from the Spirit World's tribes or a human being from a nomadic family?"

His companion replied with an alacrity that desert people would not have thought typical of nomads or of the denizens of the Spirit World, "Don't they amount to the same thing? Don't communities lose their distinguishing characteristics as dusk falls?"

"You're right. We say that too. But I can affirm I've never seen you before, despite . . . despite my intuition to the contrary."

"Now you deny with your tongue a matter you first thought certain."

"You're right. The veil confuses the matter for every eye. Thus even the most perspicacious people cannot affirm categorically that the person seen today is the same man they sat with yesterday. That happens whenever the distinctive signal provided by headgear changes."

"But wise men cannot perceive the identity of a creature who hasn't wrapped a veil round his head."

"That's most amazing."

"During raids, combatants deliberately fasten veils to fallen comrades' faces to distinguish their own fatalities from the enemy's."

"That's most amazing."

"A son of the desert emerges veiled from his mother's belly. So how would you expect the veil not to become a member of his body like his hand, shoulder, or arm? How could the veil not become one of his identifying features?"

"Is this why some tribes treat it with veneration akin to their respect for the Spirit World?"

"You said 'some tribes.' You really ought to say 'all tribes.' I don't know even one clan that doesn't worship this rag."

"Forgive me for this slip of the tongue, because the fact is that the best people of our tribe also venerate it; so much so that a group of them almost erects idols to it and offers blood sacrifices for it."

"I'm not surprised to hear this from my master's mouth, because I know in another desert another tribe that inherited from their ancestors a religious festival that honors the veil. During it they slaughter sacrificial animals, warriors race camels, and young women sing the noblest melodies. On this day, each year, there is a contest for the best-looking veil."

"But . . . but let's skip the veil's story. Tell me why you think a person in charge of public affairs shouldn't walk in public, defenseless and alone."

"Because once a person takes charge of something, he becomes sacred and is no longer considered a man."

"Did you say 'sacred,' or has my hearing deceived me?"

"Master, your hearing did not deceive you."

"How could a man change overnight, after being an unclean chap who has walked among the people?"

"Because he borrows his authority from another realm that we refer to as the Spirit World; because his is a sovereignty that mimics the ultimate sovereignty of the Spirit World."

"Spirit World?"

"Haven't you noticed that people in positions of power also disappear from public view, just like the Spirit World's authority?"

"Amazing! I hadn't thought of that before."

"The sovereign must inevitably draw two weapons: one to frighten the inhabitants of the wasteland and one to frighten the denizens of the Spirit World."

"Why should the Spirit World's inhabitants be on guard against a miserable puppet inhabiting the wasteland?"

"The sovereign is the only creature at which everyone's arrow is aimed: those of the desert's residents and those of heaven's inhabitants."

"Amazing!"

"Whenever a man's rank increases, the number of those who serve, protect, and rally round him increases. Whenever a man's status grows great, the number of amulets fastened to his neck also multiplies."

"But why should an influential person fear both visible and invisible beings?"

"Because creatures—both the invisible and the visible—always regard the sacred with worshipers' supplication. They always cling to someone venerable, whether a man walking on two feet or an enigma beckoning toward the void. The ancient disposition, the mysterious disposition, is what has decreed that man will raise his hand to wreak vengeance on the person or object he desires. The hand destroys only what the person craves. Man slays only the one he has loved."

"That's the most amazing thing I've ever heard!"

"The trick is to be wary, not to listen in amazement."

"What are you saying?"

"Hire bodyguards, tonight . . . not tomorrow."

"I once knew an important man who took charge of the people's affairs and lived among them without feeling a need to take steps to guard himself against others."

"I knew this man too, but confusing a leader who migrates through the desert with his tribe with one who takes charge of a people within the redoubts of the oasis is a grievous error."

"I won't deny that some of my peers share your opinion, but. . . ."

"That's not all. You must tax the people and set tariffs on caravans in transit."

"Slow down."

"I fear it will be rough going for a ruler who doesn't begin with this small step."

"Not so fast! Slow down."

"Take your time choosing assistants. Be on guard against hypocrites' cunning if you want to avoid mistakes."

On the horizon, the firebrand was suffocated, leaving behind an evanescent twilight. In the wasteland, the night's darkness advanced and evolved between the valley's banks into true gloom.

The wayfarer concluded even more hoarsely than before, "Our master ought to retrace his steps before the gates in the wall are closed, because we have inherited from our ancestors the belief that it's an ill omen for a bridegroom to spend his first night away from his bride."

"Did you say 'bridegroom'?"

"The ruler is also a bridegroom, and his kingdom his bride."

He thought he heard the wayfarer release a hoarse laugh muffled like the hissing of a snake, before disappearing into the retem thicket, which was enveloped in gloom, without uttering a word of farewell.

3

The oasis.

Snare for the nomad, paradise for the thirsty, treasure for the stray, and homeland for the slave.

The oasis.

It reveals itself in the vast, almighty sea of sand as a disruption. It flirts like a coquette, opening its arms to new arrivals with the seduction of a beautiful woman desiring to be possessed. It tempts with its plentiful shadows, promises the abundant water of a heavenly spring, and presents the fruit of its land lavishly, until the eternal wanderer surrenders and savors the fruit. Then the farmland of the oasis bids him tarry, detains him, and fastens him to it with a thousand pegs. It whispers in his ear, "Relax. Eat and drink. Enjoy yourself, because nomadic life brings only thirst, the unknown, and assorted terrors."

"Relax," it whispers to him. "Rely on me, because beyond my borders there is nothing but devastation and loss."

Clasped to its bosom dwell the faint of heart, those who ignore longing's song, which they receive from the wasteland's mouth as a precept they might use to discover another oasis lying beyond the wasteland.

They slumber in the dewy shadows, wallow in the muddy mires, and—instead of singing—cram their mouths full of suspect fruit that ignites in their bellies an inferno called gluttony. As slackness becomes habitual, they forget the song and lose the amulet concealed in it. Thus they cannot find their way to the maxim that prods them to search for the distant oasis lying beyond every other oasis and that warns nomads against the trap of falling into the false snares of oases that appear on the open road.

4

From the direction of the blacksmiths' market he heard a din of voices, raised in fierce debate. Foreigners' gibberish mixed with the cries of the rabble, transforming the tumult into a detestable chaos unknown in the tribe even during armed raids. Why did the ancestors curse in their maxims every form of commotion?

Why did they muzzle the mouth of anyone unable to keep still? Why did they forbid children to speak in the morning and allow them only a limited number of phrases during the remainder of the day?

Some sages find these arrangements excessive, whereas others think them a necessary strategy to train children in self-control and to force them to bridle their avid tongues from the time they leave the cradle. Their first argument in favor of this inherited suspicion of speech affirms that the head cannot think while the organ in the mouth is moving. The more the tongue's activity increases, the more sluggish the head becomes and the more its languor grows. The head's languor afflicts the heart with a malady called death. It is a death, in these people's opinion, much worse than departing from the physical world to the Spirit World's realm, an event some other tribes call death. They decided that this detestable disease afflicting the heart is the true death. For this reason, they devised a mighty punishment for people dominated by the mouth's organ and unable to refrain from chattering. They gagged these people's mouths with scraps of linen or strips of leather in the first instance. If the wretches repeated the offense and people complained about their garrulousness, the authorities would stuff their mouths with wads of palm fiber. As they attempted to speak, their jaws crunched down on the fiber, injuring their tongues and mouths, which bled as they moved through the settlement. Despite the harshness of this punishment, many people were unable to prevent themselves from chattering. They would frequently raise their concern with the nobles or even the leader. They would say that speech is not a shortcoming that requires punishment, but rather a nomad's right. The diviners—who sketched precepts for the tribes and decreed edicts saying that too much talk leads to a display of ignorance and that, where prattle abounds, prophecy disappears—did not merely restrain their own tongues, but took more life from their chests than they put in. The argument in favor of the tongue normally did not convince the wise, who reclaimed for themselves the charm, which priests had dictated, that speech repels prophecy.

When fear of losing prophecy became a concern that worried the ancients, they searched for another antidote to treat such people. Then they devised a bit (called an *asedras*) to silence chatterboxes, even before they used it to wean kids from their mothers' milk. They would pierce both jaws with fiery skewers the way they bored through a camel's muzzle. Then they would deliberately insert a wood or iron bit that pressed down on the tongue, preventing it from pursuing its wicked mission. Some obstinate people felt that to restrict speech was to restrict life, but if these wretches insisted on moving that organ in their mouths, ignoring the pain this action caused, their mouthings would be inaudible or unintelligible, a ludicrous or disgusting, muffled raving.

5

As he traversed the northern alleys leading to the blacksmiths' market, the din grew ever louder.

The din.

There are various levels of din in the oasis.

There is the din of the markets, the din of boys, the din of women on the roofs of their homes, the din of the rabble who never stop quarreling, and another eternal din that resembles the rumble of distant thunder when clouds charge in from the north. The last is a mysterious, murky din reminiscent of the Spirit World's call, heard in the murmurs of jinn tribes in the caves of Tadrart or Tassili.[3]

---

3. Tadrart Acacus and Tassili n'Ajjer, Saharan mountain ranges both recognized as UNESCO World Heritage sites because of the prehistoric rock art found there.

This mysterious din, however, dissipates when a struggle flares up. Then melodies are stifled by the screams of devotees of dispute, quarrel, and outcry.

He set off alone to hunt for the voices of the Unknown, to pray for stillness's assistance in calling to mind eternity's whispers, while here in the oasis the din abrogated inspiration and cast prophecy into the abysses of chaos. Here the nugatory absorbed detestable voices to annul the sign that the stratagems had devised to lead him and to assist him in a matter he had not himself chosen. For how could someone who had not been granted a share of wisdom, had not received a prophecy, and had never detected in himself any genius or special gift lead people unless he were alone and sought inspiration from tranquility? Didn't yesterday's leader serve as an example in this respect? Wasn't seclusion the helpmeet of all leaders and sages? How could a ruler succeed in anything while dwelling in the heart of a constant din, night and day? Wasn't tumult the destiny of oases and the din in them a sign distinguishing them from the desert?

On his way back from the wasteland, after the stranger had disappeared, he had almost perceived a secret truth. He had almost bagged an illumination about governance. Yet he had to acknowledge now that this enlightenment had also faded away. The people's voices caused it to bolt like a camel that spots the jinn's ghostly specters. Here, driven by curiosity's fire, he was endeavoring to discover what was beyond the hill. A void, a weakness, and an insinuating whisper filled his heart.

6

Out in space the light of a nascent full moon appeared. The houses' roofs and walls were illuminated by a disorienting, dawn-colored firebrand. The walls' shadows, however, extended through the alleys, assuming gigantic size and hiding the faces of the youngsters who crowded into a corner overlooking the market square to watch the group of adults huddled together in a circle a few steps away. The youngsters looked stealthily at one another, contradicted each other, and argued in loud voices, as if they were mimicking the adult gathering or had caught this infection from them, echoing their clamor. He stood above them, without anyone noticing. He faked a cough, but this was drowned in the din. Then he shouted in a loud voice, "Don't children fear that the Spirit World's specter may smother them if they wake it with their shouting?"

The huddle fell apart and some raised bare heads split by crests of hair, which in the shadows' gloom appeared ill-omened insignia traced on their heads by a fiery bar. Their silence seemed twice as profound since the din nearby was so loud.

One of them asked sarcastically, "To which specter does the specter refer?"

Some of them guffawed; others restrained their laughter.

He threatened, "In this desert lives a mighty specter unseen by the desert's eye. The specter set a condition for your ancestors to obey when they came to ask his permission to dwell in the desert. The specter said that he couldn't bear tumult and wouldn't allow his homeland to be shared by anyone who didn't know how to keep quiet and that he would stifle anyone who violated the law of stillness. So watch out!"

One of them craned his long neck, attempting to ascertain the man's features, which were not merely covered by his veil but were concealed behind veils of darkness as well. Finally, astonished, he yelled, "Who are you? Our master?"

Other voices repeated after him with respect and consternation, "Our master?"

They fled silently. They retreated on tiptoe, with bare feet, keeping their faces trained toward him until they had gone a safe distance. Then they all started to run away together while the shadows of the alleys swallowed them.

In the adjoining empty space, which was flooded by the light of the nascent full moon, the din of the other group grew louder. They clustered in a circle for a time and later separated as individuals and pairs. They crowded around a body he could not make out. They cried out loudly to one another, like herdsmen castrating a prize camel or helping him mate with a she-camel.

He stopped a few feet away and pretended to cough. Then he asked, "What's going on here?"

His question was lost in the tumult of voices. So he took a step closer before repeating it.

Some more time passed before one of the young men noticed his presence. This was a tall fellow wearing a white garment and veiled in white as well. Although he was tall, his body was rather plump, unlike that of a son of the desert.

Examining the other man in the pale light, the young man asked, "Our master?"

"Have you no shame? You've awakened the dead in their graves. Your din deafened me when I was walking in the wasteland."

"It's the jinn, master. The jinn are to blame. We found that he was hiding the forbidden metal in his pocket and wanted to bind him so we could bring him to you, but he has a jinni's power. Don't let his size deceive you, master. His arms are stronger than any warrior's."

"Is he a member of the tribe, a caravaneer, or a nomad?"

"How can we determine his community, master, when we can't even bind his wrists? How, then, can we wrest an answer from his lips and interrogate him?"

At that moment, strong men pushed forward to assault the lean body, and their garments screened him from sight. The wretch, however, shook free of them with a heroic bound. They retreated, causing each other to lose their balance and fall backward.

Standing before the crowd, he shouted, "Let him go!"

They did not, or did not obey at once. They were silent. Some of them gazed in astonishment at him. Others separated from their prey. One of them, however, continued to hold a palm-fiber rope, the end of which was tied to a wrist of the skinny body.

He repeated, "Let him go!"

They made way for him. He stood above the head of the kneeling victim who looked up at him with obstinate, gleaming eyes. The man was panting and trembling. His veil had come loose during the struggle, revealing his mouth and part of his head. He stretched out a shaky hand to rearrange the lower part, without taking his eyes off the figure standing over his head.

He said, as he gazed into the distance, as if addressing another specter, "Come with me to a private place!"

A mixture of determination, astonishment, and anxiety showed in the lean body's eyes, but the captive said nothing, nor did he attempt to flee.

He turned to the youth who still clung to the fiber rope and ordered: "Free his hand from the fetter."

The young man waved a leather purse in the air and asked testily, "But what will we do with the gold, master?"

7

They traversed a dark, stifling alley. High walls hid from him the nascent sphere's light. In the next stretch, the walls on either side were farther apart, and the depressing alley was transformed into a spacious street manacled with draped shadows. At its end, the track led to an empty area that extended to the market space reserved for caravans arriving from the west. Then it descended to the south to join the region that began at the well's mouth and ended with the thickets by the fields.

Light from the deluded sphere, which rose ever higher, flooded the empty area. The ancestors' beloved appeared pale and tired after struggling for a long time with conspirators.[4] It had finally been able to defeat these enemies from the Spirit World, even though it had lost a side of its body during the struggle.

The leader spoke as if resuming a conversation that had just been interrupted. "If you tell me the truth, I'll free you."

Hearing no response, he clarified his remarks in the same tone, "The tribe has never arrested one of its members for theft. I imagine you're not ignorant of the severe punishment that awaits anyone who doesn't merely steal another person's wealth but adds to the theft a deed even fouler."

"Another deed?"

"Have you forgotten that possession of gold is an even worse offense under the laws of the oasis?"

"I'm not responsible for bringing it into the oasis, master."

"But the young men discovered it in your pocket. So you're responsible for the metal that was in your physical possession only moments ago."

"I thought, master, you would order a splendid robe of honor for me as a reward for taking this perfidious metal from the hand of perfidy in order to rid the oasis of its evil."

"A daring argument such as this sounds like something a vassal's son would say. Do you belong to one of the tribes of vassals?"

"We are all vassals, master."

"Despite its cleverness, your argument doesn't convince me. Do you mean to say that seizure of stolen property constitutes

---

4. In Tuareg folklore, the moon is a representation of the goddess Tanit, and during different phases of the moon and eclipses she is seen as being attacked by enemies.

restoration of the rights of the original owner, not theft? Desert tribes all agree that no matter where gold has been found, it has been stolen from the tribes of the Spirit World. Did you intend to return this trust to its owners after seizing it, or did you wish to possess the gold for some other reason?"

His companion was silent for a long time. Looking vacantly at the empty land, he said enigmatically, "Forgive me, master, but this is my secret."

"You see, the Law says that a man shouldn't steal a commodity in order to return it to its rightful owners, even if they are the residents of the Spirit World. So what drove you to commit this offense?"

There was no response.

"Was it need?"

No response.

"Are you hungry?"

No response.

"The desert's miracle is that it is barren, devoid of vegetation, and may lie dormant for many years but never starves its inhabitants. What land spawned you that you should claim that hunger drove you to a deed that customary law universally condemns?"

"I affirmed to my master, moments ago, that this is my secret."

"Wretch, what secret could sanction commission of a major offense?"

"Forgive me, master."

"Fine. If you don't want to divulge your secret, tell me whose treasure it is."

"Who besides a merchant would possess gold, master?"

"Is he a local merchant or a member of a passing caravan?"

"Does my master promise to release me if I tell him the truth?"

"I started our discussion with that pledge. So tell me!"

"The owner of the treasure is the man with two veils."

"The man with two veils?"

There was no response.

"Are you referring to the chief merchant of the oasis, the man who debated leadership with Imaswan Wandarran? Is the treasure his?"

"Yes. Some people like to refer to him as the man with two veils to mock his style of veiling."

"But he has taken a place in the council of nobles because of his wealth. Is it conceivable that a man who has joined the council of nobles would violate the law of the nobles?"

"The man with two veils isn't the only one who owns gold in this oasis, master."

"What are you saying?"

"Most of the people in the oasis own gold and trade it covertly when selling and buying."

"What are you saying?"

"That includes the nobles in the council, master."

"What are you saying?"

"Everyone knows this. I fear that my master is the only one who doesn't."

"Don't you know, wretch, that possessing gold dust is a punishable offense under the law of the oasis? Don't you know that this prohibition didn't originate with the founding of the oasis but is an ancient law that recent generations have inherited from ancient ones? Don't you know that down through the generations people haven't substituted silver for gold out of asceticism but because of the prohibition that stemmed from acceptance of a pact concluded between our ancestors and their Spirit World neighbors? Don't you know that violation of the pact is a matter that will bring misfortune to the oasis and its people?"

"The slave standing before you, master, isn't the only creature who knows about the ancient covenant. Indeed, everyone knows. The nobles of the council know, first and foremost."

The leader was silent. They had reached the high fields, where scents of grass, trees, and moist earth assailed them. A scarecrow was positioned somewhere to the east. By the light of the looted sphere it looked mysterious, enchanting, real, and worthy of the legends that describe the conduct of scarecrows.

The leader said, "I vowed I wouldn't disrespect the former leader's edicts."

There was no response.

"The punishment will be inspired by the majestic nature of the Law we have inherited."

"Will my master punish the pillars of the council too if he ascertains that they hoard the infamous metal?"

"All the desert's people are equal before the desert's law."

"I fear my master may not be able to do this."

"Watch your tongue!"

"Sorry, but they possess a sovereignty that supersedes my master's."

"I don't know, wretch, from which planet you've fetched this conviction."

"From the planet Earth, master. Everyone knows that the pillars of the council are sovereign masters. If that weren't so, they wouldn't have dared to violate the prohibition against hoarding gold in their homes."

"It's certain that nothing in this desert stays hidden for long. I'll learn the truth of what you say in less time than you imagine."

"Will my master punish them if they're caught red-handed?"

"I'll administer to the tribe's nobles the very same punishment I dispense to the vassals' son if the accusation is proven against them."

"What punishment do you wish to dispense to the vassals' son?"

"The very same punishment we inherited from our forefathers: exile."

"Exile?"

"The noblest punishment for a nobleman and the harshest for a commoner."

"I don't understand."

"You'll understand some day. I mean that you won't understand exile until you've lived it. You'll depart tomorrow with the first caravan."

"Does my master mean. . . . Didn't my master promise to release me?"

"Is there any release more ultimate than exile?"

"But. . . ."

"You'll depart tomorrow with the first caravan."

Somewhere to the east, from the vicinity of the scarecrow's eerie figure, they heard a muffled sound: a suppressed, gloating laugh. Or perhaps the opposite: sobs bottled up in a chest or a phrase that had died in the throat turning into a mysterious cry. All sounds resemble each other when restrained. All contradictions resemble each other and harmonize when the subject is confused.

THE PURSE

1

In the commodities market he watched the man with two veils converse with a merchant from a caravan that had just arrived in the oasis. He asked himself at once, "I wonder what language merchants speak? Are they past masters of the language of circumlocution and indirection like desert people? Does jargon flow from their tongues—as with the people of other professions?" He realized that he had never debated merchants before. It astonished him that he was only discovering this now.

He passed a group of men who were struggling with camels laden with bundles. Livestock were stirring up dust with their hooves. In the air were diffused the smells of spices, camel dung and urine, perfumes, and dried fruit from lands to the south and north. These made him feel dizzy, because he was accustomed to recalling with each scent a murky inspiration, even if it vanished in a flash. The blend of scents today, however, far from awakening any illumination, made him feel nauseous and dizzy.

As the sun sank in the west, the walls' shadows stretched toward the east. Beyond the walls, the bleating of flocks returning from their pastures could be heard.

He stopped after several paces. The man with two veils faced his companion at times, wagging his index finger, and then bent over a sheet of leather in his other hand, while the piece of linen covering the lower half of his head shook. Then he would nod his head again to return to the animated conversation.

He advanced several steps closer and gestured with a jerk of his head toward the man, who paid no attention. He looked at him without seeing him, like someone with a troubled heart.

He took another step closer and waved at him insistently. Then the man finally stopped his chatter and approached with a troubled gait. He thought he would start with a joke. "I circled the two of you repeatedly and tried to attract your attention several times, but businessmen seem to blot out the rest of the world when together."

"Merchants can forget the world's existence but never that of rulers."

"Do businessmen have such a high regard for rulers?"

"In commerce, there is no place for high regard, master, but merchants venerate the authorities more than anyone else, because they know that commerce can't exist in a power vacuum."

"The oasis's leader is happy to hear this from the chief merchant, but tell me about caravans. Tell me about market conditions."

They walked west, encountering herds of sheep, goats, and camels with their herdsmen. Trails of dust rose from the twilight horizon, and in the open countryside shepherds' shouts mingled with the grumbling of choice camels and the bleating of wretched goat kids.

They turned south to avoid the herds and headed toward the fields. The man with two veils said, "Despite our worries, master, commerce is the noblest craft man has devised."

"Really?"

"I'll tell you the truth, master. If commerce didn't exist, death would be a hundred times easier than life."

"It's that significant?"

"I often spy on dolts who live quietly. I'm astonished they don't die of loneliness."

"If we ask these people about the mercantile life, they'll express their amazement that you all don't die from disorientation."

"They say that, master, because they haven't experienced commerce's enchantment."

"And they say you're opposed to asceticism because you haven't experienced the bliss of tranquility."

"Nonsense, master. They say the ugliest things about us, assuming that we engage in business solely to make money."

"Is there any point to business besides making money?"

"The fact is that making money is a single loop in a chain seventy yards long."

"Amazing!"

"The charm of commerce doesn't reside in the accumulation of profits but in a secret totally distinct from profit, master."

"Amazing!"

"We compete to reach this secret—not from a desire to achieve the security we imagine we earn by gaining control of a larger stash of treasures."

"Could I learn something about this secret?"

"If the tongue, master, were capable of disclosing this secret, that would make the matter much easier. Your slave, master, will give you half the riches he has spent decades accumulating, but how impossible. . . ."

"What can't the tongue disclose?"

"The tongue, master, is an organ that wasn't created to disclose information about secret mysteries. It was thrust between our jaws to veil intentions and to hide our secrets in the most remote recesses."

"I'm hearing this insight for the first time today."

"Allow me to ask my master why a beautiful woman captivates us? How can beauty rob us not only of our dignity but of our common sense as well? What's beauty's secret, master?"

"Don't expect me to say that it resides in the body, because I've seen as many beautiful women in my life as there are pebbles beneath your feet and have embraced half of them. But I only lost my senses when I met the she-jinni for whose sake I fought my comrade, the hero. I discovered in her eyes, and perhaps in her voice, the lethal sign you call a secret."

"Will it satisfy my master if I tell him commerce is like a beautiful woman? Dolts love her physical appearance. Fools are enamored of what they can see of her with their blind eyes, but the hidden aspects of her body and the veiled characteristics of her appearance are perceived only by lovers of a different stamp, lovers who don't want from commerce what she gives everyone, what she provides to amateurs, adventurers, and lucky individuals. They search for something more and pursue another secret, another treasure, greater than any other, but the miserly creature knows how to protect her treasure with a thousand talismans. Thus only disciples who pursue her for a long time will find their way to it. Only one who has shown exemplary loyalty, devoting his entire life to her, will find the path."

"Is there anything in the desert that's worth giving our lives for?"

"Yes, master: pursuit, exploration, and happiness."

"Happiness?"

"Yes, master. Commerce is good news for each day, and good news is a single day's happiness."

"Doesn't the good news turn bitter when a contract results in a loss?"

"When a contract results in losses, good news turns bitter only in the hearts of amateurs, adventurers, and lucky people. The true merchant, the businessman who has perfected his game, laughs his head off over a loss, because he knows that loss is only a sign that inevitably precedes good news. In exactly the same way, the wise jackal fills the valleys with mournful howls after eating its fill, because it knows from experience that hunger inevitably follows satiety, and fills the valleys with laughter when hungry, because it knows from experience that repletion inevitably follows hunger. The true merchant, master, understands game theory. He celebrates a day of loss and similarly is delighted by an era of glad tidings. Game theory is a second secret of commerce. Commerce, master, is like life. A person doesn't profit from it until he has lost repeatedly."

The leader looked at him stealthily, curiously observing him through the evening's gloom. As if to himself, he whispered, "I wouldn't have suspected that a creature this fond of commerce existed in the desert."

"I'm not fond of commerce because I've profited from trade. I'm fond of it because it has taught me to see it with a different eye. It has taught me that this mysterious profession isn't a pursuit of commodities in the deserts, nor the import of the rarest merchandise from the farthest countries, nor the realization of profits for parents to leave to undeserving offspring. Real commerce is, rather, like life. Commerce, master, is life! Can my master stop living because citizens consider it stressful?"

"That's actually what most people think, if not all of them. I don't know anyone who hasn't termed this profession stressful."

"Because these people have never reflected on the true nature of life. These people have never realized that life is stressful."

"Life is stressful?"

"Yes, master. Life's reality lies in this breathlessness people refer to as stress."

"That's a daring statement!"

"Every true statement is daring."

The leader was silent. His sandal sent a stone rolling while he tried to suppress his reaction. He stifled a loud groan. Then he said enigmatically, "If I were wise, I wouldn't hesitate to debate this idea with you."

"One who takes charge of people's affairs will never lack for wisdom."

"What are you saying?"

"I mean that wisdom is always leadership's partner."

"How does that apply to a leader who had no role in his selection?"

"Probably his case wouldn't differ much, because wisdom trails leadership, not vice versa."

"This view also deserves debate."

"For a man to take responsibility for people's affairs is no insignificant matter. In this mass of people, the ruler will inevitably find himself one day, because disorder, which some people consider to be inherently meaningless, is what renders a person wise."

In the evening's gloom he continued to glance inquisitively and stealthily at the other man from behind his veil.

He smiled enigmatically and said, "I wonder what you will say about leadership if you speak in the name of your beloved commerce?"

"Commerce cannot exist in a land without leadership."

"Really?"

"Leadership is the first precondition for commerce, master, because in leadership is concealed the people's law that curbs their desires. Commerce differs from other belles in her fear of desires."

"Really?"

"Sovereignty's the only specter dreaded by desires. It's the only sword that can limit the desires' tyranny. Commerce shelters in this sword's shadow."

"Bravo! Now I've perceived the secret behind your struggle to choose a leader who walks on two feet rather than one who reposes in the temple's shadows."

"Yes, I will never deny that this was the reason for my struggle."

"Tell me the truth: Were you behind the groups that came in delegations to my door?"

"I'll do more than just say yes, master. I'll go even further and say I'm proud I was behind that campaign."

"Could I know the reason for this pride?"

"Doesn't raising the status of the oasis provide a reason for pride? Doesn't the sight of caravans packing the markets provide a cause for pride? Aren't the benefits lavishly bestowed on the oasis's residents a reason to boast? The masses attribute this to you personally, master. They say that naming you leader was a good omen. But I trace the cause back to its root. I say that this news has reached merchants in the farthest countries. They feel confident that passion, which whispers to people and threatens the life of commerce, has not merely been curbed but has been returned to its flask. So they journey here, flooding through the gates of the oasis."

They crossed a brook in which water swirled. Encountering a plantation of date palms, they turned west. From the earth rose a smell of dampness, grass, and mud. In the distance the spectral scarecrow stood—enigmatic, mighty, and real. When the leader spoke, his voice carried far away, sounding inscrutable, as if the scarecrow, of whom the oasis's people told legends, were speaking. "We have learned the place of leadership in commerce's soul. The time has come for us to learn the place of gold in this realm's customary law."

"I'll mention an opinion that in the past I have shared with some companions. Today I think that there's no reason to hide it from my master. If leadership's sovereignty is the sword behind which commerce shelters, then gold dust, master, is the spirit of commerce."

"Now I'm hearing an opinion more daring than any other."

"I want you to hear the truth that no one else will tell you, master. I want to inform you that it has been a fatal mistake from the start to forbid transactions in gold."

"Not so fast! Slow down!"

"In the council, you all have always based your arguments on the ancient Law's precepts, forgetting that the Law was never a legal code for oases but merely the customary law of a desert that has never recognized commerce and is even unfamiliar with trade, because life in its expanses is too primitive for all this. But in the case of oases the situation must differ greatly. Oases require respect for different laws, because they make up a different world, one that doesn't merely differ from the wasteland but is the exact opposite of the desert. These laws have sanctioned commerce and made trade a reason to live. If in the oases we have believed that commerce is a secret of life, we must necessarily have thought that gold dust is a secret behind commerce."

"Why does every people agree that gold is an ignoble metal that—with its arrival—transforms a land's finest people to its basest?"

"That's because the people discussing this, master, have been nomads, moving through barren lands bereft of anything but mirage and sky. Those people fear gold dust, because they fear commerce. They fear commerce because they fear stress."

"Now you're close to disaster. Now you're circling the ghoul's cave. Beware!"

"Yes, I know I'm standing at the edge of the abyss. I know I'll be forced to say something reprehensible, but I'll say what must be said. I'll say that your people flee life by fleeing from commerce and from gold, as if fleeing from a plague."

"Bravo! Bravo!"

"In the desert peoples' blood courses an odious enmity to life."

"I've been expecting to see you tumble into this pit for the last hour."

"I don't feel embarrassed, master. The desert's inhabitants are the born enemies of life."

The leader stopped and gazed at the nearby specter of the scarecrow. He asked sternly, "Is this conviction your reason for twisting the stick in the Law's hand and hoarding gold in your house despite the prohibition?"

The man with two veils also studied the enigmatic specter and then checked the upper fastening of his veil with his fingers. He responded with the firmness of someone expecting this accusation, "I didn't hide the gold in order to speculate with it in hard times the way some members of my fraternity do. I have held on to it as a trust for a dear companion who left it in my safekeeping."

"Really?"

"As you see, I haven't violated the Law in any way, because the precepts forbidding possession of gold also encourage us to respect a trust and to return it to the rightful owner, even if we realize that these assets include gold ingots."

"What a wily schemer you are!"

"The embargo notwithstanding, the day when owning gold will change from being a cause for suspicion to a cause for pride is near at hand, master."

"How can you be so sure?"

"Commerce, not I, is sure about this. I wanted to say that you all will recognize gold, if not today, then tomorrow, because you won't be able to accept commerce and reject its spirit."

"What a sneak you are!"

"Forgive me, master, but I'm still waiting for the trust."

"What did you say?"

"Your slave hasn't received the trust that wretch seized."

"Do you really expect me to return the purse full of coins to you?"

"Does my master intend to seize people's goods? Does my master intend to retain the assets of others?"

"But I'm not the one who revealed the assets' secret. I'm not the person who told people that the purse contains a pile of gold."

"My master shouldn't forget that the law of trusts supersedes all others. My master shouldn't forget that the legal system decrees that a trust should be returned to its owner, even if it is gold."

"Can you persuade the oasis's inhabitants that this is true?"

"Persuading people is the responsibility of the responsible person."

"What are you saying?"

"I mean to say that addressing the masses is entirely my master's responsibility."

"What a shrewd schemer you are!"

"I just want to return the property to its owners."

"It's out of the question that what you consider a legal property should be returned to those you consider its owners, after everyone has learned the true nature of the serpent that the purse conceals."

"My master is making a mistake!"

"What are you saying?"

"My master isn't merely injuring my rights or those of the owner, but the rights of the Law too."

"Speaking for myself, I say regretfully that after seizing the purse and its contraband contents, I cannot restore it to someone who deliberately attempted to conceal it from other people."

"My master's making a mistake."

"Is this a threat?"

The chief merchant did not reply. Darkness overwhelmed the fields and stillness dominated the area, causing the spectral scarecrow to look even more august and eerie. They retraced their steps silently, their feet sinking into the muddy mires. A muffled sound rose behind them: a mocking, suppressed laugh, a sob of lament, or a phrase so choked in a throat that it emerged as an indistinct cry.

All sounds resemble each other when muffled.

All opposites seem concordant when a matter is confused.

THE CAMPAIGN

1

He chose them carefully. He chose men immune to ecstasy, men unaffected by yearning when they listened to melodies celebrating the full moon's arrival. They were men who had never been observed to lower modesty's wing in the presence of women or nobles. They had not passionately endeavored to retire with beautiful female jinn into the caves of the chain of blue mountains.

He chose the men with the toughest souls and the most ruggedly intrepid bodies, gathering them in a retreat where he addressed them in a mellifluous voice as if reciting verses of a satirical poem. "Know that we don't combat the metal of misfortunes because it has, since the most ancient times, been a harbinger of chaos and that we're not setting forth today to expel it from our homes out of loyalty to the ancient covenant that our ancestors concluded with the jinn tribes. We embark on today's offensive with the sole aim of defending ourselves, because even youngsters know that this ill-omened metal's arrival inevitably devastates a land and turns its most distinguished citizens into the most abject. Will you sanction a disgrace in your homes that you wouldn't wish on your worst enemies? Will you allow your souls to be humiliated by the forbidden dust in a way that you wouldn't accept even from yourselves? Shall we violate a law that each generation has inherited from the previous one and submit to the wishes of greedy people in order to satisfy insatiable bellies?" He also discussed timing, the best moments to begin, and the importance of surprise. He counseled them to reconnoiter and to beware of underestimating tricky strategies and extolled secrecy at length, concluding that it was the key to the affair's success. When he raised his right hand toward the heavens, his disciples understood that this gesture marked the campaign's beginning.

2

The man with two veils was granted permission to enter. His protruding cheeks looked pale. The leader saw true anxiety in the man's eyes. Behind the fading pastel double veils he detected concern.

This concern was soon voiced.

The chief merchant stopped at the entrance and cast him a rather threatening look. In a voice strained by anger, he said, "I thought we had agreed that day."

"Agreed?"

"I thought you agreed with me when I told you that commerce is a maiden who becomes beautiful only in the shade of a sovereign's sword. How can you have forsaken me today and slain her with that same sword?"

He smiled and gestured for his guest to sit beside him. The pallor of the man's cheeks increased. He sighed deeply, and the sound resembled a serpent's hiss. He told his guest, "Today you resemble an angry child. It's not seemly for a rational adult to lose his balance, even if he sees raiders kidnap his beautiful maiden."

"If only the men kidnapping the belle today had been raiders from hostile tribes! Enemies from marauding tribes kidnap. Internal enemies slaughter!"

"I'm grieved to hear you assert that an agreement was reached between us merely because I tried to listen to you like a friend."

"I thought words differed little from food."

"I don't catch your drift."

"When a wayfarer meets you in the wasteland and nourishes your heart with a secret that assists you in coping with the terrors of the route, isn't this secret more precious than the morsel of food he places in your knapsack as provender?"

"I'll grant you that."

"Then why have you betrayed a tongue that informed you of something no one else had?"

"I wasn't trying to entice you to say anything you didn't wish to say."

"But you know that the organ housed between the jaws cannot be restrained, even by its master, once it has been set free."

"Is a man blamed for a defect that originates in human nature?"

"A secret, master, is a covenant, and you're the one who enticed me to talk about the state of the caravans and to discuss commerce's secret."

"Did you suppose I would wait for commerce's secrets to be revealed before launching an attack on the metal of misfortunes?"

"But the attack on gold was an attack on commerce. Or did the words' gist escape my master that day?"

"The fact is, I don't remember much of what was said."

"In any event, it's out of the question for noblemen to disdain the trust for which my master was responsible."

"You're still talking about the trust and the covenant."

"You didn't merely reveal my secret, you harmed the entire oasis by profiting from your knowledge of the secret."

"Today, you not only resemble a child, but you're even talking like a kid who has lost his puppet."

"On many occasions a man must channel the obstinacy of childhood when defending himself. A man must on many occasions borrow childhood's tongue to dare to speak the truth."

He rubbed his hands together, smiled enigmatically, and said contemptuously, "Fine. What recompense does childhood ask in exchange for freeing the rational adult from error?"

The man with two veils replied with childish obstinacy, "My master would do well to end the campaign."

"End the campaign?"

"Today, not tomorrow."

"This truly is childish!"

"My master will help himself first of all and secondly will benefit other people."

"Is this a threat?"

"My master would be well-advised to act quickly before the suffering becomes even more widespread."

The lower section of his veil slipped, revealing his lips. Then his host saw spittle trickling from them. He also noticed that his guest was trembling violently and suspected that he heard the man's teeth chattering and clacking as if he were racked by fever. The pallor of the man's projecting cheeks faded as a murky color suffused them. The man's eyes narrowed and eyelids with irregular blue creases, which bulged out like tiny vipers, unfolded.

3

The leader swayed before his companion as if overwhelmed by yearning. He released the painful groan that springs from the chests of deranged people before ecstasy transports them to alternative realms. He moaned for a long time before he repeated, as if reciting a sad song, "Even you, companion of eternity! Even you, son of nobles! Even you, warrior hero!"

Ahallum, however, replied in a tongue uninfluenced by ecstatic people's magical incantations, "Gold is the destiny of oases. Why don't you accept this fact?"

The leader began to sway back and forth, lowering his veil over his eyes. He asked mellifluously, "How can you expect me to accept a matter that violates the Law? How can you ask me to profane the precepts of our forefathers?"

"We left our forefathers in the wasteland's tombs. Now we inhabit oases. Today we're Waw's children. The wastelands have a legal code and the oases another. Why don't you want to acknowledge that?"

"How can you ask me to acknowledge a matter that is calamitous, according to our precepts? Do I know more than our forefathers? Are you shrewder than our original grandfathers?"

"Our grandfathers didn't tie themselves to the land. In their endless migrations they didn't practice commerce."

"What need does a nomad have for commerce? What need do caravans of migrants have for goods?"

"This is the problem: you don't want to acknowledge that we haven't been nomads for a long time. You don't want to admit that we've been bound to the land for forty years. You've forgotten the Law's precept saying that to stay for more than forty days in one place is a mark of bondage to the land. What if the number forty modifies years, not days?"

"Anyone who ties himself to the earth becomes the earth's slave. Any slave of the earth finds himself exchanging goods for a profit and becomes a merchant. Anyone who adopts commerce for his profession acquires the dust of misfortunes. Isn't this what you're trying to have me believe? Isn't that what seduced you into hiding the hateful metal in your house?"

"Yes. I'll never deny that I—like all the nobles—have smuggled gold dust into my home. I smuggled it in not because I yielded to its beauty, which enslaves women and weak-willed men, but because its possession affords security."

"Security?"

"Yes, master. Gold dust in the owner's hand is a gift of security. Gold dust is life's secret for everyone who chooses agricultural land for a homeland."

"I'm amazed by what I hear!"

"This isn't just my opinion; this is what all the nobles think. This is the opinion of the entire population of the oasis, including the person closest to you."

"What are you saying?"

"I'm saying that gold was seized in your only daughter's residence too."

"No!"

"Didn't the vassals tell you that?"

"No!"

"Now you've finally learned that your adversary is a specter found in every home in the oasis. It has dared invade your household too."

He began to sway back and forth again, releasing his pain in a new moan. Ahallum asked, "Do you still consider the people's sweetheart an enemy?"

The leader released a deep sound as if intoning an agonizing tune. His companion inquired, "Are you going to persist in plundering houses and destroying the metal?"

The leader began to tremble but did not reply.

4

That evening Imaswan Wandarran also visited.

He sat down on an expertly tanned leather mat, which lacked the typical colored wool embroidery and which was spread over a thick goat-hair kilim rug placed beside the wall.

The mixed-race maid brought in froth-topped camel milk in a wooden mug. He took the mug with both hands and gazed at the froth, which was slowly dissipating. Then he placed the mug on the leather mat. He listened to the froth's whispering as it continued to disappear. He deliberately violated circumspection's rituals. "If the goal of the campaign was to inform people of your majestic rule, then rest assured that you've succeeded. If the goal was to raise respect for the Law, then know that this lost constitution never ordered the violation of what people conceal in their hearts or homes. Have you finally realized that everything has a proper limit?"

The leader watched him inquisitively. He asked in an artificially complacent tone, "Is this the council's advice or a warning?"

"It isn't the council's custom to warn those it has recommended for leadership, even though our customary law also affirms that those in power shouldn't adopt a position the council hasn't authorized."

"I beg your pardon. It's just that over the last few days I've grown accustomed to hearing a threat in the words of all those who have sat in this same corner."

"If I were in your position, I would have excused them, since I wouldn't know what to expect from people whose possessions and reputations have been assailed."

"Answer one question for me: Why did you all select me from among yourselves if you didn't mean for the leader to be the Law's guardian even more than the people's ruler?"

"The fact is that we never chose you. You know the hoi polloi selected you."

"The rabble?"

"The problem is actually not the rabble's choice, since the rabble have never been good at choosing, given that they never know what they are doing or what they want. The true affliction, however, has been your credulity."

The leader waited for him to complete his statement, but the guest fell silent and went back to contemplating the vanishing froth in the mug of milk.

So he asked sternly, "In what sense have I been credulous?"

The guest responded casually, "You believed you really were a leader!"

"Who am I, by your lights, if not a leader?"

He retorted harshly, "You're a puppet!"

"A puppet?"

"Didn't you hear them say from the beginning that they couldn't bear to be led by a leader who reposed in a sepulcher and instead wanted a leader from the earth's residents: a puppet that walks on two feet?"

"That was a typical circumlocution. That was a linguistic trick to hide the meaning. You're the first to take this literally."

"Our master is mistaken if he believes so. The masses say exactly what they mean. Even when they intend to speak circumspectly, as you suggest, they fail and express themselves bluntly."

"What are you saying?"

"I'm trying to say that you committed a fatal error when you believed the lie and assumed that you could be a real leader instead of a puppet."

"Here again I discern a threat! Admit immediately that you're threatening me!"

"They wanted you to be their puppet like all the other political stooges, but you rushed to draw your sword the moment they handed you the sovereign's mace."

"What do you all want from me? Why don't you reclaim your sovereignty if you want a puppet? Why don't you release me?"

"I fear, master, it's too late for that now. To save the situation, you can backtrack and accept a puppet's costume, like any other puppet."

The leader's chest resonated with his sorrowful moan. Looking up at the ceiling of palm fronds woven around palm branches, he said, "I'm afraid that ever since you chose the wrong man, thinking that anyone can don a puppet's veils, it has been too late."

"Am I hearing an opinion or receiving a decision?"

"If it is a decision, it's destiny's."

"I'm sorry to hear this."

He looked at the elements of the ceiling's fabric and was astonished by the regularity of the rows of branches and the delicate weave of the palm fronds. The workmanship was comparable to a beautiful woman's beadwork stitched onto a saddle cloth she has embroidered for a beloved warrior.

When he looked down again, he saw that the froth had vanished, although the mug was still full. The guest's spot, on the leather mat, however, was vacant.

THE PUNISHMENT

1

The next day the specter appeared in the walled alleyways, walked some steps beside him, and then said in the same husky voice as before, as if continuing their previous conversation, "You've collected vassals to assist you but have forgotten the bodyguards."

"Bodyguards?"

"Didn't I tell you that bodyguards are an amulet for sovereigns' brows?"

"I actually don't remember. But . . . who are you?"

"Now you abandon the momentous matter to chase after your curiosity the way worldly people do."

"Did you say 'momentous matter'?"

"Yes. When a man elevates worldly affairs while neglecting his own soul, he abandons momentous matters."

"What do you mean?"

"Know that you possess nothing in the world besides your soul. If you don't create a fortress for it, you'll have only yourself to blame."

"Are you speaking in a threatening way too?"

"No, I'm telling you to defend yourself against the threat."

"But you want me to commit a heresy that no desert leader has yet committed."

"You forget that you're not a desert leader. You forget that you live among people who changed out their hearts by soiling their feet in their fields' mires, by settling in houses, by turning metal into coins in the blacksmiths' market, by allowing consumer goods to seduce them in the caravans' markets, by acquiring gold dust from merchants and crafting from it jewelry to use to purchase maidens' hearts. . . ."

"Not so fast! Slow down! Behavior like this doesn't transform a person's nature. A man doesn't change into a ghoul overnight."

"My master thinks well of creatures. But my master should beware, because such elevated opinions are deadly."

"Deadly?"

"What matters to me is warning you."

"I would feel embarrassed walking among the people surrounded by bodyguards."

"Life is a gift more precious than specious shame, master."

"Do you think the danger is this severe?"

"Life is a gift more precious than specious shame, master."

While he traversed the eastern alleys that ran parallel to the blacksmiths' market, the man was beside him. When the alleys ended at the temple plaza, however, he found that his companion had disappeared, as if the alleys' shadows, which had spat him out, had returned to swallow him.

2

Shivering is not a typical reaction to danger, but it does suggest anxiety: a nameless anguish shackled by distress that drives one to panic, so that the afflicted person finds no room for himself.

He had felt panic-stricken for days. He could not sleep and felt ill at ease. So he fled to the wasteland to search for a cure. Prior to these panic attacks, while drifting between sleep and wakefulness, he had seen a snake. Taking this to be an ill omen, he had drawn from his kit an amulet to protect himself against evil. He added this to the necklace of talismans he wore. Now he proceeded through the empty land while attempting to recall the vision. He had seen the serpent stretched out in the shade of a retem tree and had walked a few steps closer. It was as long as an arm, svelte, clad in a rough skin, like the ridges in a lizard's tail, and dotted with vile, loathsome, venomous spots that provoked a shudder and revulsion. He had found the sight entrancing and bent down over the creature. Armies of ants crawled around it; so he felt sure it was dead. He wanted to bury it and fetched a stick from a nearby tree. He lifted it with the end of this piece of wood, but it escaped after he took a couple of steps. As it slithered down, it touched his index finger. During that momentary contact, it struck him indolently with its fang. So he threw down the stick. In its eyes he saw a hostile, resentful, enigmatic look—a nameless look that said, "Have you forgotten that I don't die? Have you forgotten that I'm called 'The Snake'?" Although this look was hideous, the serpent's gaze was rather slothful and indifferent. He examined the nick on his finger and discovered that it was bleeding. He started to shake and perspire, sensing that he was becoming feverish. Before the fever took hold, he had awakened to find his body bathed in perspiration and his limbs trembling. What did it mean for the reptile that had been a rotting corpse to return to life? What secret lay behind this lazy bite that had made him bleed?

He loitered in the wasteland for a time and brooded at length. Then he went to a diviner who had arrived from the forestlands the year before and erected a straw hut near the blacksmiths' market.

The fetish priest listened to the vision indifferently and then commented just as lackadaisically, "This vision isn't worth a trip to a diviner. In our country, even children can explain prophecies like these. I'm astonished that you haven't recognized that the serpent represents an enemy. You'll be exposed to an enemy's cunning. So beware!" He started to leave, but the diviner called after him, "This world, master, is nothing but a den of vipers. The serpents in question are the people closest to us. If you want to be safe, don't let any comrade out of your sight."

3

That evening, the vassals came to discuss tariffs and the caravan traffic and to recount news of the tribes, foreign lands, and markets. Asen'fru, the tax administrator, commenced, saying that news of the campaign against gold had been carried by the jinn and thus had reached the lands to the south and the kingdoms to the north. Many merchants had ordered their caravans to change routes and bypass Waw. He affirmed, however, that the situation was not as grave as claimed by the oasis's nobles, whose commerce had been injured by the attack, because the markets were still flooded with goods that surpassed the needs of the oasis, and the taxes collected from farmers, blacksmiths, shop owners, and professionals still showered the treasury with plentiful riches. Then, rubbing together coarse hands caked with a dry crust like a lizard's scales, he concluded his presentation with the suggestion: "If my master would order the exchange of the gold that comes from the oasis's inhabitants for pieces of silver from passing caravans, the wealth that would saturate the oasis would bring its people unprecedented prosperity."

He exchanged a quick look with the chief vassal and also glanced at the campaign's commander. Then, leaning forward, he ran the palm of one hand over the back of the other. The scales contracted into grim ridges with a distressing sound but relaxed once the palm of his hand passed by, and then settled once more into depressing gray lines.

Abanaban, the chief vassal, asked, "But will this prosperity last long if the oasis loses the confidence of the caravan trade?"

Although he spoke in a distinguished style well suited to a nobleman of the council, he had never been admitted to the council, despite belonging to one of the tribe's most ancient lineages, despite the esteem in which his clan was held by the tribe's other clans, and despite his wisdom, reputation, and the influence he exerted over other people.

The tax collector immediately replied, "Exchanging the confiscated gold for silver will suffice us until we develop a strategy to rebuild the merchants' confidence and until we restore the caravan trade to the oasis."

Tayetti, commander of the campaign, interjected, "Restoring the confidence of businesses that have left will take longer than optimists expect. So beware!"

He was the shortest, smallest, and plumpest of the men sitting there, but his impetuosity, passion, and precipitous speech and his body, which quivered while he spoke, showed he was also the most zealous. The oasis's rabble assumed that the leader had chosen him to lead the campaign precisely for these traits. Abanaban inquired with the nonchalance typical of dignified ceremonial behavior, "Why these suspicions?"

The campaign commander's whole body went into convulsions. He thrust his neck forward, and his entire body tensed and plunged after his neck, making it seem to the group that he was about to leap into the leader's arms. In a voice that revealed both passion and certainty, he declared, "Commerce is like a runaway camel. Once it bolts, recapturing it won't be easy. I hope you don't forget this!"

The vassals exchanged discreet glances. Whenever they looked stealthily at one another, they turned just as covertly toward the leader to search for some clue in his eyes. The leader, who had been listening aloofly to them throughout, finally asked in a suspicious tone: "Who mentioned the noblemen's caravans in this council?"

The vassals exchanged glances again—glances that suggested astonishment, doubt, and scorn.

The tax collector said, "I did, master."

"Why?"

"I wanted to say what everyone knows, master. I mean, the matter has been public knowledge for a long time."

"Which members of the council have sponsored a caravan?"

"All of them, master. The most recent is Amasis the Younger, who sold camels and slaves to send a caravan to the northern kingdoms."

"You said Amasis the Younger?"

"He's the latest, master. That's why he's been hit the hardest."

"Why didn't I hear about this before today?"

"We thought you would know more about it than anyone else, master, because it's common knowledge."

"Amazing!"

Again the vassals exchanged glances; then the leader repeated distantly, "Amazing!"

The vassals' eyes revealed their astonishment, doubt, and scorn.

4

He was tormented by insomnia again that night.

The next morning his anxiety evolved into a lump in his throat as hard as dry dirt. Feeling nauseous, he tried to vomit. He went to Retem Valley, where he wandered for a time. Then he lay down beneath a bushy retem tree with branches decorated with new buds dripping sap. Northern breezes caressed them, making them quiver and sing. The weeping branches, which curved down, traced arcane designs like the symbols sorcerers inscribe on leather amulets.

He studied the signs on the ground and looked at the flower buds spreading down the branches. The mysterious buds reminded him of beads in an enchanting necklace on a beautiful woman's neck.

He also listened carefully to the music.

The north wind was blowing intermittently in determined gusts. The branches responded with an energetic, communal dance, swaying in every direction like a group of ecstatic people, pulling back at times and then joining together before moaning a yearning melody.

Suddenly, in a nearby thicket, another melody broke forth.

This tune scared off the retem's, stifling that other song. The valley's stillness was violated, and the desert was menaced by disorder, because whenever the Spirit World's bird sings for people in the valleys' groves, a prophecy is embedded in its songs.

He sat up and straightened himself to listen hard and long to the melody. He observed the emptiness for a long time. The song of yearning in the retem branches was silenced. He told himself out loud, "This is an ill omen! This is a calamity!"

That evening, in a dark corner, an enemy stabbed him.

5

That evening, on his return from the shops, in the dark of an alley, a ruffian attacked him, plunging a ferocious knife into him with an apparently lethal and brutal thrust.

The first blow was the most forceful, striking him in the left side of the thorax, but his leather necklace of amulets blocked the blade's tip, preventing the knife from finding its way to his heart. Then . . . then other blows followed that first strike—he did not know how many, because he blacked out immediately and did not regain consciousness for several days. He awoke to find the herbalist standing over his head, waving a necklace of amulets and saying, "Who can deny the power of amulets after this? Had it not been for these charms, master, the criminal would have slain you with the first blow. So learn from this!"

That evening the nobles visited him and sat on the kilim rug by the wall. They said a lot. They spoke, but he did not hear, understand, or respond to their questions with a single word. He lay on the other side of the room, by the opposite wall, wrapped in blankets. He felt nauseous and struggled to resist pain and unconsciousness by focusing on the remarkable craftsmanship of the handwoven palm-branch ceiling.

The noblemen left and the vassals entered.

They stayed for some time, chatting, but he did not hear, understand, or employ his jaws' organ to speak a single word. So they fell silent and departed.

But . . . but a single specter remained huddled in the home's right-hand corner—silent, dejected, and enveloped in stillness and darkness, taking no part in the discussion and not even opening its mouth to ask a question. It watched the invalid with lackluster eyes, closing them occasionally from exhaustion and pain only to open them again obstinately and inquisitively. At some point, when he did not know whether it was night or day, he found himself addressing a blunt question to his mysterious guest, "Who are you?"

The visitor did not reply and continued to hunch over its knees, clinging to its eternal silence.

He waited till the maid appeared to ask who the man was. She leaned over his ear to whisper, "He said he's a comrade of my master's. We found him in that corner, master, the first day of the calamity. He hasn't eaten, moved, or spoken with the other visitors. Master, he's an odd specter."

6

Some days later a group of noblemen appeared.

They came by night. The vassals left immediately. The nobles sat by the wall in an awe-inspiring row and began the ritual with a lengthy silence. He realized immediately from this act that they had plotted something.

Slaves brought them cups of milk and platters of dates, but they clung to their stillness like a group of jinn. In the other corner, a specter hid, hunched over, recoiling till it almost became part of the wall.

Finally, the hero began, "We've come today to bring our master good news."

He fell silent, and stillness returned, dominating the dwelling for a time. Ahallum then explained, "I mean to inform my master that we have been able to arrest, finally, the person who dared raise the criminal blade over my master's head."

He cast an inquisitive glance at him. So the hero asked, "Does our master remember the day he sentenced an oasis wretch to banishment in the desert?"

The leader's sudden interest was obvious. So the warrior looked round at the nobles' faces and then continued, "Didn't my master ask the wretch back then why he had raised an iniquitous hand and stolen from the homes of immigrants a purse accepted as a trust?"

The leader shook his turban no in response to this suggestion. Then Ahallum explained, "My master doesn't know that the wretch's only reason for the theft was the lord of all reasons in the desert."

He fell silent. Eventually, he declared, "A beautiful woman!"

The leader exclaimed involuntarily, "A beauty!"

"Yes, master. A beautiful woman is the cause. The wretch had fallen in love with a girl who had lost both parents. Her guardian was a disgusting woman, a distant relative. The wretch had asked the guardian for her hand in marriage, but the old woman exploited the girl's beauty to humiliate the young man, requesting such a large sum of money that the lover could only acquire it by theft. After our master banished him from the oasis to punish his foul deed, he returned secretly to the settlement and tried to seize his beloved by brute force. His plot might have succeeded had the guards not cleverly stopped him at the last moment and pulled his poor beloved out of the sack. Then the rascal fled once more, but the wily schemer wasn't content with this abominable deed and returned some days later to take his beloved to eternity."

He fell silent. The leader gazed at him in astonishment and asked vacantly, "What are you saying?"

"I mean to say that he slaughtered her, master. He slew her and with the same knife sliced off her right breast before fleeing again."

"What are you saying?"

"He fled but returned, the way he had each time, because his thirst for revenge would not be slaked till he stabbed the person he held responsible for the calamity."

"What are you saying?"

"He came back to stab our master, feeling certain that you had caused his suffering when you seized the purse of gold from him."

"No!"

"We finally found him lurking in the groves in the fields. So we shackled his hands and locked him up. Tomorrow, in public, he'll receive his punishment."

"An unbelievable story. A tale fit for ancient storytellers."

Ahallum exchanged a long, strange, enigmatic look with the chief merchant.

A naughty smile glinted in Imaswan Wandarran's eyes. In the corner, by the wall, a muffled, evil, hoarse laugh—like a serpent's hiss—reverberated.

THE WRETCH

1

The leader's wretchedness was excruciating.

The leader did not know that, had the wretch been granted a choice, he would have chosen exile over any other homeland. The leader did not know that exile is a punishment only for inhabitants of oases and fainthearted desert dwellers. The leader did not know he had sentenced him to dwell in the other Waw, the original Waw, the real Waw, not the distorted Waw that tribesmen ironically, maliciously, and derisively referred to by this lofty name. The leader did not know. The leader, like all other leaders, was the last to understand that had it not been for the poor creature he left behind in the oasis imprisoned by crumbling structures, the wretch would not have returned and the miserable walls would not have received even a last farewell look from him.

But the beloved changed everything.

The beloved woman changed the desert paradise into a place of exile. His true love converted crumbling walls into a paradise. His true love transformed the real Waw into a despised exile and made the fraudulent Waw seem a heavenly oasis. This ordinary creature would not have been able to perform this magic, this ghostly figure would not have been able to turn the desert upside down, had she been a creature like any other, had she been a beautiful woman like all the others. She was, however, a belle from a different community, a creature from another lineage, and a ghostly figure of another temperament, because she reciprocated her lover's love.

A belle in love appropriates the female jinn's potential and turns the desert head over heels. A man who loves a beautiful woman appropriates the secret of the male jinn and in his pursuit of his true love turns the desert upside down.

2

He did not capture her heart by mastering poetry, the way Lotharios are wont to do, and did not win her affections with his brawn, since his mates had criticized his physique and had even sarcastically and derisively nicknamed him "Grasshopper." He did not take her with the edge of his sword or by any feat of heroism, because he had not received from the heavens any of these attributes. Thus he was not amazed when he fell in love, but he was astonished when his love was returned. How, after all this, did they expect him to fall in love and then forget his true love, the way most lovers did? How could they expect him to refrain from loving his true love a second time and even a thousand times?

3

Yes, yes . . . he fell in love with her and she loved him too and reciprocated his affection. Then he decided to reward her love with eternal affection and to repay her love a thousand times. He roamed the open countryside for a long time before discovering a ploy. He withdrew from society for a lengthy period while he consorted with Barbary sheep, gazelles, and desert lizards. He settled as a neighbor to the Spirit World's residents and conversed with the jinn's priestesses and the Spiritual Kingdoms' sages before he discovered the talisman and returned to share with her the glad tidings that were his prophecy. He told her he had absented himself for a long time to search for an answer to her question about what it meant for a person to love someone a thousand times over. Then she wept with longing and recited verses to him about her desire to hear this prophecy. He wept too and told her he had heard the mountain peaks, the jinn's priestesses, and the body language of all the beasts repeat a single phrase in response to this question. He told her that the desert's creatures had all agreed that loving someone a thousand times means living as if the only being in the desert of whom you are conscious is your beloved.

Oh! If only the Spirit World had granted him poetry's muse, he would have recited the most exquisite verses about how captivating it is to love someone a thousand times.

4

En route to his thousandfold love, however, he inevitably encountered a ghoul.

It was not an ordinary desert ghoul but a unique type of ghoul previously unknown in the desert's history. The ghoul was one of a kind, because thousandfold love is unique, as his ancestors had told him in tales. Unlike all the other ghouls, the one that stands guard over thousandfold love cannot be slain by a hero's sword. It is the sole ghoul that can only be vanquished with treasure, because it safeguards treasure.

The ancestors had warned him about this in their tales too.

5

He set out to gain control of the treasure that would free his thousandfold love from the ghoul's imprisonment.

The jinn whispered in his breast, and the voices of all creation repeated the jinn's refrain. The wind hissed the talisman's secret in his ear. They told him that he would never succeed in gaining the treasure unless he possessed the amulet known as strategic planning. They also told him that this treasure was itself the fruit of strategic planning and that for this reason it would be necessary to rely on strategy to reclaim its offspring.

When he investigated, he realized that caravans traversed the continent, crossing the desert from each of the four directions, bringing from the north loads that were put down en route in oases to exchange for local produce. Then they proceeded further south and marketed their goods within the forestlands' borders. There they exchanged merchandise from northern and central kingdoms for that coquettish dust. Then they returned by the same route with their find. In the markets of the oases they would display part of their stash, and wizardlike artisans and men with furnaces and hammers would seize the opportunity to transform this dust into gold and to shape the gold into jewelry and coins. Thus the metal increased in brilliance, beauty, and sordidness. The merchants carried their new commodity, their lethal wares, goods that are the only motivation for any conspiracy, the sole reason for which a woman would deceive her mate, a brother would raise a hand to slay his brother, or a prophecy would die on a diviner's lips. They proceeded with their terrifying wares that had been transformed by wily smiths into a genuine treasure they could proffer as they stormed the central oases and northern kingdoms. He witnessed how it slipped into the oasis and studied the way it drove people insane, disturbing residents' minds and stripping wisdom from the heads of the wisest sages. He saw its impact on people and believed in its power. Its magic convulsed him, and he began to tremble anxiously whenever he witnessed its gleam. He heard disquieting voices repeat the refrain that the secret's wares were the market's destiny. Then someone appeared who claimed these goods were the destiny of oases. Finally, propagandists went even further and avowed that the secret's wares were life itself. Then he nearly choked in distress, and slipped away from the strongholds of the oasis as though fleeing from a ghoul.

The ghoul standing guard over her treasure, however, eventually forced him to plunge into her strongholds. The ghoul standing guard over her treasure demanded a treasure in exchange for releasing her treasure to him, because a treasure is required to buy treasure, and the only way to escape from the ghoul is to seek refuge with the ghoul.

6

Two days before he burst into the ghoul's cave, he stole into his beloved's house. There he found the guardian hovering around her ward's chamber like a she-demon from the wilds. She gestured to the woman that they wanted to be alone; the crone cast her a threatening look before retreating behind the wall. That night she told him the schemer had decided to grant him only forty days to bring her what she demanded. If luck did not favor him, she would consider herself absolved of her promise and would sell the girl to the owner of a shop for hides and linen in the blacksmiths' market.

This was a despicable proviso from a despicable creature, but it would not have unnerved him so much had he not seen in his wretched true love's eyes a lethal pain he at first thought he had never seen before in a living creature. Then this pain reminded him of the eloquent expression in the eyes of a gazelle kid he had surprised in a Barbary-sheep gulch. He had grabbed hold of it with both hands, and it had resisted him for a very long time, trying to escape. When it finally gave up and started shivering silently, he had seen the same expression and the same pain he now witnessed in his beloved's eyes. It was a look of impotence born of a loss of strength and power and of desperate surrender that discounted any deliverance short of a miracle. It was a pain that surpassed other pains, a despair greater than other types of despair, and a surrender beyond other forms of surrender. What was the significance of this look? What should a person call this type of pain? Was it a calamity or something even greater than that? Yes, yes . . . in the gazelle's eyes and in his beloved's was something even greater than a calamity, because it contained some of the Spirit World's majesty, the certainty of recluses, the purity of those who expect no boon or beneficence from the world or from worldly people. In it, regardless of everything, there was a mysterious rapture washed with prophecy's nectar. He bolted from the house as if a snake had bitten him and then slipped into the ghoul's cave.

7

He saw nothing, felt nothing, and thought nothing till they seized him.

Within him stirred a beast he had never encountered before. It flew him to the treasure's abode the way the jinn fly desert prophets to the desert's end. This was a bold soul mate. In its impetuosity, zeal, and nonchalance, he detected the daring of a person who has taken charge of some matter, any matter, oblivious to any shame that might accrue should the matter go awry. He asked himself at once about the provenance of such a soul mate in a desert where the Law disapproves of daring. A man there must inevitably mull over every issue a thousand times and question the diviner time and again before taking a single step forward followed by a step back, in order to overcome at last the whispered insinuations. When he decides to throw his full weight into the struggle, he discovers—too late—that the combat has ended, that the dust has settled, and that only the battle's debris is left on the field. The reason for this behavior is not a fear of loss. It is, rather, an ancient, age-old dread of the ghoul named dishonor. For this reason he was amazed by the impetuosity of this mysterious soul mate and felt certain, beyond a doubt, that it was a creature from another lineage not affiliated in the slightest fashion with those of the wasteland.

This brute, who excited his admiration and whose feats and heroic deeds astonished him, left him, however, and disappeared the moment he was arrested.

8

They cast him before the leader, who sentenced him to banishment.

He set forth with the first caravan, and they dropped him off in a harsh, dead, lethal patch before the next oasis, because the law governing banishments decrees that the condemned person should not serve his exile in another oasis after he has been convicted of a crime in the previous one. They left him in a deadly wasteland with water, dates, and some barley and continued on their way. He walked along with the caravan for a distance and then stood watching till it reached the horizon, where a mirage swooped toward it, tearing it limb from limb.

He wandered through the open terrain, which was strewn with rough stones of comparable height and size. These were copper-colored and scattered across expanses stretching in all four directions, limited only by horizons swamped by the tails of mischievous mirages. No rise of earth burst from the plain and there were no dips. There was no hint of a hill and no promise in the distance of a mountain or an acacia. As far as the eye could see, the earth's surface did not decline downward in a gulch or ravine and showed no willingness to reveal any hint of life through a blade of grass or even a dry tuft of weeds. It did not provide the least indication of good will. Indeed, to the contrary, it confronted him—scowling, threatening, and hostile—the way it does any wretched stranger ignorant of its secret. However, it is absurd to think that the desert's ruses would dupe a creature born of the desert. It is absurd to think that a mother would deceive a son whom she had carried in her belly, fondled at her breast, and borne on her back. It is absurd to think that the ruse would trick a being whose entire training in strategies was provided by the desert, whose only passion in life was for the desert, whose first and only world was the desert, a person who never recognized a flesh-and-blood mother until the desert granted him permission, because she was not a mate, a mother, or a beloved. A creature who was not part of the desert but the desert itself—could this being defile the law of existence and plot against himself? Would he accept—like doltish travelers—that what he saw was what recluses refer to as annihilation? Would he believe that the first mother might one day reject her ancient offspring and cast before him snares woven from death's ropes? Would he not be the first to know for certain that what seemed to outsiders a scowl was actually a smile, that what fools deemed sternness was diffidence on her part, and that what terrified strangers in her hostile expression was actually a promise and a renewal of a covenant? Did she not once tell him that she is a belle who gives herself only to those who have been faithful to the covenant and who only find themselves and discover their lost spirits when they rely on her and unite with her?

9

He rushed off, trailing the playful liquid that bubbles up in the wasteland to tempt fools, strangers, and masters of ignorance. He pursued it for a day and a half and spent the night in the heart of the obstinate maze that spreads and extends in every direction without ever promising anything. He passed the night but did not lose heart. Indeed, to the contrary, his smile never left his lips while he stretched out on his back, lying in wait for information from the life of storms. He was spying on the desert and listening to her mysterious voice. She was menacing her prodigal son—as was her wont. She was chiding the son who had ignored her and had followed the tribes that adopted houses not unlike stone prisons for their residences. She threatened, browbeat, and brandished the penalty in his face.

He listened humbly to the anger of this most ancient of mothers but smiled surreptitiously and enigmatically, because he knew this language in the same way he knew the mirage's trajectory. He knew the language of mothers. He also knew the hearts of mothers. He knew that the language of mothers is one thing and the hearts of mothers are something else. He knew that strangers, or even relatives, grow angry and then hurt you when they threaten. He knew that only a mother instructs when she threatens or punishes; so he smiled. He smiled at the wretchedness of the deluded and began to read his mother's messages in the stars' trajectory, because she had once taught him to read her reports in the heavens' storms, in the prevailing tendencies of the Qibli, or in the murmurs of the Spirit World's inhabitants. He carried his reading to the extreme. The Camel captivated him and he followed behind her until he spotted the Calf fastened by a weak thread spun from colored wool. The poor fellow was hungry and thirsty for the mother's teat, and the mother was inflamed by longing for the Calf, but for the mother to meet the Calf would cause the destruction of the desert and the heavens. The Calf's escape from the wool tether is the mothers' extinction and the sons' annihilation. Can fragile wool thread prevent the Calf from escaping? Will the mother bear separation from the Calf for long? Or—were the sorcerers right when they declared that the era when a thirsty calf takes the camel's dug, when the Camel consents to meet him, is our own era, the era of us creatures of dust, because in the law of the higher spheres, this era lasts no longer than the wink of an eye, whereas in our reckoning it seems a timeless eternity?

He discerned the sign in the sphere. He received a prophecy from the history of the Camel and the Calf. He perceived the omen and realized that the immortal mother would on the morrow open her arms to him.

In the morning he picked up his meager provisions and set forth before the sun could surprise him.

He did not change course the way careless people would. Instead he chose the same direction he had selected the day before, because setting a new course is an error the desert will not forgive. In the wasteland's language, insistence on a new route is called oscillation, hesitation, loitering, and walking in place. A traveler who wishes to reach a destination does not circle around an area unless he wants to become that area's prisoner. An area's prisoner is not called a traveler in the desert's customary law; he has become a stray.

Overhead, the sun's tyranny persisted. In the barren land the mirage's floods spilled forth, but the eternal, copper-colored wasteland was intolerant and unyielding and did not waive its threat. Into its immortal expanse a new sign descended. In its severe calm a new signal appeared. In the wasteland, in its competition with itself, with its rough body, which continues endlessly and never stops regenerating itself, a new prophecy appeared, borrowing a new veil woven from hurtful indifference. This indifference, which ignored beings and mocked the fates of creatures, paid no heed to whether those afflicted were people or livestock. This indifference is a snare for strays, because it terrifies and disorients them, making them feel desperate. Then they defeat themselves, because they submit to their destinies even before those destinies have judged them. The latent cause is always their ignorance of the desert's modus operandi. These wretched intruders do not know that when the desert dons a veil of indifference this is a sign of contrition. If the naked landscape disguises itself and hides behind indifference, then the exile, which is multiplied and threatens to endure, struggles against the banished man's death agony.

He smiled mischievously beneath his veil and surrendered to the expanse the way dry weeds surrender to the wind's assault or the way straw yields to an unruly flood. He abandoned himself to allow the naked land to lead him to any country it wished. He allowed himself to become the naked land's pawn, because he knew that the noble wasteland would never renege on a covenant made with a person who surrendered himself as its hostage. He had learned that—from time immemorial—progress through the desert has been like swimming through water, like floating in the spring-fed ponds of oases. You must relax and give your body totally to the water if you want to stay afloat. In the desert, too, arrogant people who act obstinately succumb. In the desert those who think they have been granted enormous knowledge and who therefore debate and resist will perish. The desert takes vengeance on this group with its labyrinth. The other group, those who surrender control to the wasteland and seek the desert's protection against the desert, survives.

10

His assumption was not mistaken.

At midday, the labyrinth suddenly fell away and he found himself overlooking the lip of an expansive, deep valley. The side from which he had approached was a very high, mountainous cliff, and the far side of the valley was too distant for him to see. In the flat land at the bottom he not only observed dense trees, which twisted through gentle valleys that curved as they ran south, but caught sight of areas covered with plentiful, intensely green grass. These spread along the borders of the clefts in magnificent swaths and encroached on the sides of the gentle valleys that branched off from the main valley, the far side of which was out of sight.

Exile died, and paradise came into view.

With the skill of a Barbary sheep, he descended from the craggy summit, and the scent of flowers, moisture, and fresh grass greeted his nostrils. Overcome by a trancelike vertigo, he thought about the miraculous desert clouds that baffle even the most cunning shepherds—where they originate, how they collect, what route they follow, where they empty their load, or in which sky they then dissipate. These experts not only do not understand the clouds' nature but are amazed by their ability to flaunt the law of the seasons, because they pay no attention to whether it is winter or summer, spring or fall. They hold back in winter when people expect them, denying their blessing, while generously bestowing their rainfall in a season when sunshine is at its most searing, as in summer. Thus aged shepherds clap their hands together to announce their incompetence when they exclaim, "Not even the wiliest diviner can predict the course of the desert's rains."

The paradise where the immortal wasteland ended, the paradise that appeared suddenly in the abyss at his feet, was also a gift of the uncanny desert clouds.

11

He roamed through his paradise for days and nights. In the low-lying lands across the gulches leading down to the ravines, he plucked the fruits of this paradise. He found delicious truffles that made him forget his banishment and propelled him into kingdoms that one rarely reaches, sees, or even contemplates.

In the valleys he ambushed lizards, hunted hares, and gathered eggs from birds.

On the mountainous cliff faces he located caverns that contained pools flooded with running water.

The leader had sent him into exile, and then the most compassionate mother of all transformed his place of exile into a paradise.

He reveled in this gift, enjoying the stillness of his isolation. So he felt happy. Deeming himself content, he committed an offense that everyone savoring the taste of contentment inevitably commits. He raised his voice in worried songs and awakened in those uncharted areas the thousandfold love. It did not merely wake up; it intoxicated him as if he were in a trance. So he found himself trembling ecstatically and struggled with his fever, as if possessed. The carpet of grass disappeared from the slopes and the trees vanished from the valley bottoms. The earth swallowed the truffles, and the gazelles, lizards, hares, and every sort of bird fled from the area. The waters of the pools tucked into the caverns of the cliff faces evaporated, as this paradise turned into a tenebrous abyss.

He resisted for a time. He butted the boulders with his head for days. He charged through desolate wastes as if the jinn had possessed him. He thought he might outstrip his belly's ghoul by racing, but these measures kindled the flame and the fever's fire continued unabated. So he shot off running and continued running, running, and running. He did not stop running until the walls of the oasis halted him.

THE CONSPIRACY

1

He did not consider what he would do until the gate brought him up short. He did not think about the process that had brought him back from the lands of exile till he was slipping into the fields, pushing between trees like a madman. He did not premeditate anything. In the shadows of his affliction he sought no burning ember, because he did not wish to discover in the prisons of despair any fissure that would show the way. After he had left, he had surrendered his affairs to the desert, and the noblest of mothers had provided his heart a carefree indifference—the immortal nonchalance that destroys living creatures, terminates the migrant, eradicates passion, and also exiles the desert from the desert. The desert annihilates itself and watches the wasteland's creatures from its new homeland in annihilation. Then no one believes any longer that there is an existence for the desert in the desert. No one believes any longer that anyone can traverse a desert that has no place in it for the desert. So the traveler, finally, doubts his own existence and soon migrates to the vicinity of the desert, in annihilation's homeland, to become a cranny in extinction's edifice.[5]

The traveler vanishes at times when the desert is veiled by indifference's scarf, but passion refuses to keep company with indifference. The desert thinks that with indifference it eradicates passion the way it eradicates living creatures, but passion—like the serpent—is not eradicated and does not vanish. There is only one way to slay the serpent: to cut off its head. Passion, however, persists, even headless. It is possible to slay the passionate lover this

---

5. Islamic mystics have used similar language—words like annihilation— in describing their quest to submit personal volition to God's will.

way. It is also possible to deliver a coup de grâce to the beloved, but there's no way to slay the passion. What is headless does not die, because a headless person does not vanish.

Tribal poets say this about a single passion. So what might they say if they discovered a thousandfold passion? Will they not believe, as I do, that the Spirit World, which is incapable of slaying even once a single passion, will be incapable of slaying a thousandfold passion a thousand times?

2

He hid in the fields till the curtains of darkness fell. Then he slipped out and entered the alleys. He concealed himself in a corner of the yard, waiting for the guardian to leave on a visit to a neighbor or to run an errand, but the despicable demon did not emerge. From his hiding place he listened intently but at first heard only the rumpus of children in nearby alleyways. He transformed his whole body into attentive ears and discerned inside the house a faint murmur but could not make out the voices. He pushed on the outside door but found it bolted from the inside. He inspected the yard's wall on the alley side but found it was hard and smooth, without any sign of a bulge that might help him climb it. He turned the other way and checked the wall on the side parallel to the buildings down the neighboring alley, discovering that here the wall was shorter. In fact, it became increasingly insignificant the farther back it went. At the far corner, the wall was not only less substantial but rougher and more neglected as well. He climbed the wall and scaled it easily. He leapt to the inner courtyard, where he saw the treasure's guard by the light of the fire next to the house's door, which was ajar. She was tending a cauldron set on three stones, adding a stick to the fire at times and then returning to lean over the garment piled on her lap in order to favor herself—and perhaps the beloved, who was squirreled away in one of the house's corners—with incomprehensible crooning.

He hugged the wall, cleaving to it till he became part of it. He scrutinized the she-demon: she truly was demonic. Her face was marked by deep wrinkles that rent her entire visage, increasing in width as they neared her "trussed" mouth, which was wrapped with another bandage of creases even uglier and more objectionable. Her hooked nose was also coated by a network of lines that resembled the protuberant veins that climbed up her face to encircle her sunken eyes and disguise her features until her whole head seemed to be a block covered by tree bark.

She stopped crooning and moaned an ancient melody. Her thread escaped from the eye of her needle, which she attempted to rethread, struggling for a long time. Then in an anxious and desperate motion, she thrust it toward her companion. At that moment he saw her. At that instant he saw her shadow as if he were seeing her for the first time. At that moment he saw his thousandfold beloved. At that moment a feverish ecstasy possessed him, and he perceived in an exalted flash—like sparks of illumination or a glowing ember of prophecy—that he had been created solely to become the mate of the thousandfold beloved and that the only reason she had been born was to become his. He also perceived that neither the desert's laws nor the heavens' fates could alter this situation and separate two creatures who had from the beginning, from before they were born, been a single being in two bodies.

3

He told her, once they were alone, that he had failed to acquire the treasure and that all they could do was flee. She replied in a tone unaffected by girlish shyness, "Do what you will." He lifted her to his shoulders and carried her through the dark alleys once the oasis slumbered. He took the route beside the wall on the eastern side, avoiding the guards of the western and southern gates. He entered the fields and constructed a ladder from palm trunks. He probably would have succeeded had he not been denounced by the eerie scarecrow about whose conduct the oasis people recount legendary tales.

Today he realized that it had certainly never been a scarecrow. It was, rather, an unruly type of jinni wrapped in a scarecrow's rags, for he heard a suppressed snicker the moment he finished preparing the trunks and was ready to take flight. This became a hideous chortle that rattled in the chest, sounding like repulsive keening—fit for the spawn of the Spirit World. The insane guffaw did not last long, however, because a commotion followed on its heels, swallowing every other sound. This was a mixture of human clamor, the cries of herdsmen, the chattering of the populace, and a disagreeable shriek like the braying of a donkey. The commotion did not merely cause the walls to vibrate but shook the entire oasis. His terror at what he heard lasted until the guards surprised him and grabbed hold of him.

He did not grasp what happened next.

He remembered only that he broke free before they had conveyed the couple to the first alley. He bolted to the walls, reached the shadows, and then the gloom of the alleyways swallowed him.

When he slipped into her house some nights later, he heard from her lips the same charm: "Do what you will."

He came to her after losing a sense of whether it was day or night. His struggle with mankind had left him dizzy; his quarrel with the fates had gotten the best of him, and fever, thirst, and fasting had exhausted him.

He came, but not the way he always had before. He did not bat an eyelid. His body did not feel feverish. There was no crazed look in his eye. He came like a ghost, crowding into the corner like any stranger. With eyes that did not even recognize her, he gazed at her by the light of the fire burning in the hearth.Was this a desperate person's submission, the tranquility of a recluse, or the determination of a hero anticipating his final battle?

He said in a barely audible voice, "I've come for the last time."

She replied in the same whisper, "I knew you would."

"But I'll never come again."

She did not respond.

"Will you come with me?"

"I've always come with you. I've always been with you."

"If I don't take you today, the skin merchant will take you tomorrow."

"I know. He has made preparations to take me even faster than you think."

"Are you coming with me?"

"Yes."

"Now?"

"Yes."

"Forever?"

"Yes."

A gleam sparkled in his eye—a strange gleam. Was it a spark of inspiration? A flash of prophecy? The omen of an earthquake? This flash glowed with a sign unfamiliar to mankind. For this reason it would have struck terror into the hearts of even the jinn.

The gleam vanished, however. Immense submission returned to pulse through his eyes.

He whispered, "I haven't wanted to do anything you don't agree to."

"I know."

"The skin dealer won't take you if you come."

"I know."

"No one will ever take you."

"I know."

"Your guardian, the leader, and the guards won't bring you back."

"I know."

"Neither mankind nor the jinn will acquire you."

"I know."

"We'll again become the single being we once were."

Before she could murmur her "I know," he left his corner quietly, and the look in his eyes blended submission, nobility, affliction, and certainty. He stood over her and removed the scarf from her head. He caressed the plaits of her hair with a cold, steady hand, which seemed an iron rod, not the palm of a thousandfold lover. He knelt down and with his other hand fondled her swelling breast, which tilted up, taut, like a bow. This hand was cold as well, but steady. Then he took her head with both hands and gazed into her eyes with the same stern look combining submission, nobility, affliction, and certainty. He stroked her entrancing neck and her right earlobe before his fingers slipped forward to close her eyelids. He trembled with a sudden shiver, but this passed, because his hands moved to her neck and clamped round her throat with an insane, eternal, iron grip.

She did not shudder or emit any death rattle. She did not experience the pains of a final death agony, because the two hands the commoners had likened to a jinni's the day they seized him were better suited to achieving this objective than a sword thrust or a dagger blow.

4

This time he did not flee.

This time he did not have recourse to flight, because he saw no reason to flee. He had fled on the previous occasions not to escape punishment, not to enjoy freedom, but because he wanted to return, to seize an opportune moment to win his thousandfold beloved. Today, after he had realized his dream and gained the bride of eternity for eternity, his reason for struggling had been eliminated and his reasons for fleeing had vanished. So he walked on his own two feet to the guards and asked them to fetter his hands.

They shut him up in a dark place for days before they finally led him to the interrogation.

In the temple plaza, the citizens had gathered. On a hill beside the temple's sanctuary, the chief merchant sat on a leather mat. Around him hovered nobles, guards, and vassals.

They brought him to a halt in front of the twin-veiled man, who began the interrogation. The wily fellow gazed at the setting sun and looked up as if searching the naked heavens for inspiration or a prophecy. He asked with a coolness inappropriate for the hideousness of the alleged crime, "Tell us first of all what you did to the girl."

He looked around the area and saw that the alleys continued to spew forth bands of curiosity seekers as the crowds grew more congested. He replied just as coolly, "I did what I had been destined to do. I mean to say that I merely undertook to recoup what I lost one day."

"Wretch, what did you lose one day?"

"I lost the creature my master refers to as 'the girl.'"

"What are you saying?"

"I retrieved her from your hands. I retrieved her so that no eye could fall upon her. I hid her so she would remain out of sight. I took her from your hands by force; for this reason I understand my master's anger, since people can't bear defeat. People never forgive a victor his victory, even if they realize they will acquire something from his triumph."

The man with two veils wagged a finger at him. "Watch out! We haven't come to listen to you discuss what people can and can't bear. We've come to hear you answer a question. So, again: beware!"

The temple plaza was still, even though it was packed with people. In the distance, at the mouths of the alleys leading to the plaza, children were making a ruckus.

The chief merchant asked, "You said you took the girl. But you didn't say where you concealed her!"

"Master, she's with me. With me for eternity."

"If what you claim is true, why don't we see the poor girl beside you."

"Because . . . because my master is blind, like everyone else."

"Blind?"

"Master, we're once again, as we were one day, a single person."

"Wretch, what day are you talking about?"

"A day before we were born."

"What is this prattle?"

"I answered my master's question."

"But why did you remove the poor girl's breast with a sword and conceal it in a feedbag?"

"I never removed a breast and have never in my life carried a sword."

The man with two veils gestured to a guardsman, who took a step forward and removed a chunk of flesh from a bloody feedbag. It was tender-skinned and quivering. Dried blood and grains of sand had adhered to its underside. He waved it in the air, and the crowd responded with a suppressed snarl.

The accused man, however, was not shaken. He neither denied nor confessed the deed. In fact, it seemed he was not paying attention, because there was no change in his nonchalant gaze into the void.

The chief merchant resumed the interrogation. "Someone who has confessed to killing the beauty with his own hands would not find it difficult to seize the breast to take as a trophy the way tribes in the forestlands take their enemies' heads. Isn't this your secret, wretch?"

"I never removed the breast."

"Didn't you stab the leader to avenge yourself because he sentenced you to banishment to punish you for your first offense?"

"I didn't stab the leader and I didn't remove the breast."

"Why did you stab the leader?"

"I owe the leader a payment for his benefaction, not an ungrateful stab wound."

"Wretch, explain yourself."

"Had I not left my beloved behind, the leader's banishment would have been the noblest benefaction and I would never have violated his sentence by returning to the oasis."

"But you did return, more than once, after that."

"I returned to retrieve a creature with whom I had once formed a single person."

"Here we're borrowing words from a fool's lexicon again."

At that moment the crowds were convulsed and people spread the news—like women gossiping—that a messenger from the leader was coming. This news spread quickly and reached the hill's summit before the messenger did. Then the chief merchant leapt to his feet and gestured to a vassal, who drew his sword and advanced toward the lover. At that same moment the man with the feedbag sprang forward and knocked the turban from the victim's head with a single blow. The bared head revealed a strange, small face, like a frog's, crowned by a long braid coiled in a heap at the top of his skull. Cries resounded in the crowd, but the man with two veils gestured again sternly, and the man with the feedbag grasped the braid with his free hand. The swordsman's weapon gleamed in the rays of the setting sun and then people saw the puny, headless body fall to the ground while the head, which resembled a frog's face, remained grasped by the man, who brandished it on high. It was bathed by the rays of the setting sun, and people saw in its eyes the serenity of a slaughtered animal. Blood dripped from the bottom of the head, falling plentifully over the feedbag where the quivering breast was tucked.

THE GAME

1

The previous day, the serpent had invaded his solitude again.

It had emerged from a crack in the wall of an impregnable cave, and he had prodded it playfully with a stick. Its puny size deceived him, and he thought he would torment it a little before smashing its head. But the ignoble reptile leapt toward his lap and would have bitten him had he not jumped to one side just then. He saw two fangs in its mouth and remembered the ancients' counsels that cautioned against small creatures, warning that snakes, like other animals, are all the more vicious and evil the smaller they are. As he started to shake, he attacked it with a cudgel. It did not succumb easily despite his desperate blows. When it finally died and he saw that its hateful body resembled a discarded rope, he stretched out beside it to catch his breath. He lay on his back and looked at the ancients' pictures on the cave's ceiling. He journeyed far away with these creatures. Some men wore strange round turbans with feathers on top, and other men—with bodies camouflaged by animal skins and long tails trailing behind them—were hunting Barbary sheep. Giant women had generous breasts. Pygmy-like figures held arrows, spears, and other weapons.

He went a great distance with his ancestors and then fell asleep, or nearly. He actually did fall asleep because he did not notice the fearful body's emanation from the Unknown, the wall, or the puny body he had slain with the cudgel. He returned from his journey to find above his head a viper cloaked in burnished scales, threatening him with three, four . . . countless heads, each containing fangs more vicious than wild beasts' tusks.

He tried to move to one side, but the reptile pursued him with its heads. So he stirred. He stirred to find the maid above him.

Placing a container of milk beside him, she asked, "Has my master had a dream?"

"I wish it had been a dream."

Adjusting his position, he noticed that he was still short of breath and that his body was wet with perspiration. Then he told the maid, "It . . . was a nightmare."

"There's nothing strange about that. An invalid inevitably dreams and perhaps has nightmares. You're still sick, master."

He wanted to tell her about his vision and gestured for her to stay. He asked, "What do they say in your tribes if a man sees a snake when unconscious?"

Her concern showed in her eyes. She asked excitedly, "Did my master kill a snake?"

"The truth is, I don't know. I thought I had killed it when I beat it mercilessly, but then I dozed off and roamed on a distant journey with the ancients. A hideous hissing woke me and I saw over my head a multi-headed viper. . . ."

"This is a horrendous evil, master."

"Is that what they think in your tribe?"

"Did my master cut off the first snake's head?"

"The truth is that I didn't."

"This is an enormous mistake, master."

"Do they say that in your tribe?"

"In our tribe, a man never kills a snake unless he cuts off its head and buries it far away. The snake's an enemy that isn't killed by beating, master."

"The diviner also told me that it represents an enemy."

"The small snake is a small enemy. The viper is a large enemy, master."

"Do they really say that in your tribe?"

"My master must be extremely careful."

He noticed that she was trembling. She bit her lip hard and fastened her scarf tighter around her head to hide her anxiety.

2

The chief vassal visited him.

He spoke for a long time about conditions but did not mention the wretch.

Realizing that Abanaban was deliberately skirting this story, he wanted to chase down the secret. He toyed with the nap of the leather mat before saying, "Yesterday I sent the campaign's commander to bring me the wretch, but he reached the gathering too late."

His companion also sought relief in the floor mat and replied tersely, "I know."

"It's said that the chief merchant ordered him beheaded before the interrogation was concluded."

"I've heard that too. . . ."

"It's said he did that to prevent the prisoner from falling into my hands."

There was no response.

"I know you always avoid meddling in the council's affairs, but you ought to know, too, that magnanimity has frequently caused the destruction of the innocent."

"I don't catch my master's drift."

"I'm trying to say that you kept silent about the many evils committed by the council because of your magnanimity. Have you forgotten that you're the chief vassal?"

"I acknowledge that I'm wary of intervening in the council's affairs because of my respect for the Law that established tribal councils in the earliest times."

"You can honor the Law in a council that honors the Law, but is it right for you to honor a council that doesn't hesitate to attack the Law every day?"

There was no response.

"I wanted to tell you that I spoke with the wretch the day he committed the crime. It wasn't difficult for me to understand the man. I say for certain now that the assassination attempt against me was totally out of character for a man like that."

"I acknowledge that many people share my master's suspicion."

"Tell me, then: Who granted the chief merchant authority over the destinies of men and allowed him to issue verdicts against people?"

"I don't know, master. We reached the temple plaza and found him seated on the hill like a bogeyman, surrounded by a vanguard of noblemen and vassals. It's said the council chose him."

"How could the council appoint the man with two veils to arbitrate a case in which he had a vested interest?"

"I don't catch my master's drift."

"Doesn't the council know that the chief merchant was the wretch's enemy? Have you all forgotten that I sentenced the wretch to exile for absconding with a purse that belonged to the man with two veils?"

"It's a truly shameful situation."

"It's not merely shameful, it's suspicious. My intuition is that there's a conspiracy afoot."

"But my master shouldn't forget that he would have received the death penalty in any event."

"How can you be so sure?"

"Didn't the wretch slay the beauty?"

"Didn't you hear they were acting to fulfill a vow?"

"That's what people say."

"Didn't he say in the interrogation that he did what he did to retrieve a creature he had lost?"

"My master almost seems to have been there with us."

"Didn't he also say he didn't cut off a breast and didn't stab a leader?"

"My master almost seems to have been there with us."

"How do you know I wasn't? Do you suppose I pay no attention to people's affairs? Don't you know that the jinn relay news to leaders' ears?"

"Our clan says that too."

Feeling drained, he paused. He was not merely panting; he realized he was also trembling. He toyed with the edges of the leather mat. Ripping off some fuzz with sudden violence, he said cryptically, "I don't want you to think too well of me."

"I don't grasp the wisdom of my master's statement."

"I meant to say that I don't merely feel the punishment was unfair to the wretch and hardly a victory for justice, but I was trying to defend myself too."

"What need should my master have to defend himself? Aren't we all my master's soldiers and guards?"

"You refuse to admit that the blows to my chest didn't come from the wretch who was beheaded. Those blows sprang from a deceitful plot."

"Who would gain anything from a deceitful plot against my master?"

"You should have addressed this question to the men who were so quick to sever the wretch's neck to prevent him from falling into my custody."

"Amazing!"

"I don't need the mind of a diviner to grasp that, after attempting to convince me of his alleged hostility, the council didn't want me to question the wretch."

"Amazing!"

"You know the ancient stratagem a wily schemer uses to convince an inattentive person of a false tale. He recounts a true story—I mean the first part is true. Then he crams the second part full of falsehoods. This type of confusion is required to render the tale credible."

Then the leader looked up at him with inscrutable, wretched eyes that released barely visible tears.

3

The day the leader had set to meet the people after his long convalescence, he discovered that groups had been gathering outside since morning, after closing their own doors behind them, in more massive throngs than the oasis had ever witnessed. Men elbowed each other aside, and women with children in tow jostled against them. Foreign residents, the masters of passing caravans, and bands of slaves formed an awe-inspiring ring around the area. The moment the leader appeared—encircled by vassals—women began to trill and shaykhs advanced, embracing him at length. He made his way through the congestion, heading for the temple plaza. Those in the crowd with special pleas rushed toward him, blocking his way. A woman began to complain about her husband, and an old man wept before him, alleging that his only son wanted to kill him because of a disagreement about a tract of farmland. A third person butted in to complain that another man had stolen his wife while he was away, traveling with a caravan. People surrounded him on all sides, and he could go no farther until the vassals intervened. He promised the people, however, that he would attend to their needs once the meeting with the nobles in the sanctuary was adjourned. He was not content merely to reassure the masses, but summoned the herald and ordered him to tell everyone he planned to address them about the campaign, metals, and the future of commercial transactions in the oasis's markets. While the herald rushed off to make the rounds of the squares and to traverse the alleys, shouting his new tidings and summoning people to gather in the temple plaza, the priest from the forestlands emerged from his miserable hut beside the blacksmiths' market and hastened toward the leader's home. The maid told him that her master had just left, surrounded by more people than she had ever seen. The diviner interrupted her, saying that she must find a way to coax him to return home as quickly as possible. When she asked why, the diviner toyed with the cowries strung around his neck. Then he told her nonchalantly that he doubted she would ever see her master in his house again if she did not succeed in bringing him home at once.

She was floored by his tone and stood watching him rush off in the opposite direction, away from the throngs. He disappeared behind the buildings along the road that led to the fields. She told herself that she had never known a diviner, sorcerer, or any other individual involved with the occult who was not eccentric. She leaned over the bedcovers and then began to drag them to the courtyard to shake off the dust and to air them in the sunshine. She was humming an ancient tune she often relied on to revitalize herself and to energize her body. How delightful are melodies and how fine are lyrics that inflame sorrows! What would have happened to the desert and its people had they not inherited sorrowful poems from the mouths of their ancestors? What would have become of the desert and its people if the wasteland had lacked the antidote and the malady both called "yearning"? Yearning is the only secret that harbors its opposite within itself. It scorches the breasts of lovers with pains till they consider it a malady. When it dies in their hearts, the loss torments them and the privation slays them. Then they realize that it was an antidote. But God forbid that yearning be consumed without poetry's flint stone to spark the fire! Poetry not only serves as a flint for longing's fire; it is also the flint stone for everything in the desert. Were it not for poetry's flint, the heart of a beautiful woman would never throb with passion. Were it not for poetry's flint, thunder would not rumble in the sky to announce the thirsty earth's inundation with rain. Were it not for poetry's flint, real flint would not spark fire.

She remembered some funeral dirges.

The ghost of poetry cast her into the ocean of the epic that tribal poets had begun but not yet concluded. All poets have shared—just as warriors on fine camels all share in a race—in reciting an epic for eternity concerning thousandfold love. She had heard from neighbor women touching verses and from chatterboxes disturbing news about the conspiracy. They had said that the beloved woman's death and her wretched true love's beheading were not the end but the beginning of a catastrophe for the oasis. Their tongues had also relayed strange insinuations. From the prattle, her ears had plucked suggestions that the leader was in danger. Yes, the elderly neighbor woman, who spoke like a priest revealing a prophecy, had said that the leader. . . . But what relationship was there between old women's gossip and the prophecy of the priest from the forestlands? Was it merely a coincidence that she heard today from the mouth of a forest priest—couched in allegorical language—the same information she had heard yesterday from a local priestess?

She cringed, cowering for a long time. Then she bolted for the door and raced through the alleyways toward the temple plaza.

4

Meanwhile, the specter was heroically battling the throngs as he attempted to reach the leader.

The congestion became even more intense near the foot of the mount adjacent to the sanctuary, because the herald's cries had sparked curiosity in people's souls. Groups poured out of houses, shops, markets, and even the fields. The vassals and guards who formed a protective buffer around the leader failed in their attempt to keep these groups at bay. People pressed his hands to congratulate him on his recovery. Some protested harsh taxes. Others deplored his attack on their treasures. Still other men declared their approval of the campaign and their hopes that he would keep up the good work. The specter fought bravely but the crowds proved stronger. Every time he pressed forward, arms shoved him back. Thus each time he thought he had advanced a few steps, he was actually a step further removed from his comrade.

The leader reached the temple door, and the circle around him became denser and more agitated. The specter made a heroic effort, but the common folk, who thought he was trying to get ahead of them to present a petition to the head of state before they could, were quick to treat him with a roughness not devoid of hatred. One of them whacked him with an elbow and another landed a fierce punch below his navel. So he screamed with pain.

Desperate, he shouted, but the clamor swallowed his cry. So he fell back on his final weapon and drew from his pocket a carefully folded piece of leather and waved it over the people's heads, shouting to the leader, who finally noticed him—he thought. Perhaps he even recognized him, because the specter saw in his eyes the hint of a smile before he raised his hands to catch the leather sheet. He threw it to the leader, who caught it with both hands. He bent over it for an instant and would have spread it out to read had it not been for the crowd's pressure. He folded it up and kept it in his hands. The specter screamed as loudly as he could, referring to the document, "Read it, master. Read!"

No one could tell whether this call, which resembled a cry for help, had reached the leader's ears late that morning or if it had been drowned out by clamorous voices. Griots agree, however, that the whole crowd heard the final, grief-stricken call, for which the specter was only a conduit, because it could easily have been a heavenly revelation: "Master, you must read it now. You must read it before you enter that door!"

The leader, however, had disappeared through the door, and the guards formed an eternal barrier between him and the people.

The instant the leader disappeared into the temple, the maid arrived at a gallop.

5

Inside the oblation chamber, once he had chosen a place among his peers, he joked, "A council of nobles wouldn't really be a council of nobles if the meeting weren't held in an oblation chamber."

Imaswan Wandarran exchanged a secret glance with the warrior. Amasis the Younger said in a strange voice, "You're right. You're doubly right."

"It's appropriate for us to slaughter a sacrificial animal in honor of the leader of the Law's return after a lengthy absence from his sanctuary."

The warrior said with unusual zeal, "We'll slay a sacrificial animal for the Law's advocate; our master can be sure of that."

"But why don't I see the council's treasure at the center of the council?"

They exchanged looks fraught with meaning. The chief merchant said in a disparaging tone, "The 'treasure of the council' can't sit up anymore. Our master should remember that the treasure is more than 140 years old."

"We'll visit him directly, tomorrow. If the council's treasure doesn't come to the council, the council must visit the council's treasure."

Silence prevailed. Outside, the people's commotion mixed with the herald's cry. The noblemen exchanged stealthy glances. The leader suggested, "We'd best begin."

They responded, almost in unison, "We'd best begin."

The hero drew an elegant dagger from his robe, pulled the blade from the scabbard, and began to rotate it in his hands. The leader protested, "I thought we agreed a long time ago to ban weapons from the sanctuary."

There was a brief silence. Bodies trembled in anticipation. Then Ahallum replied with unusual coldness, "How does our master expect us to slay a sacrificial victim to honor the sanctuary's authority if we don't bring a dagger into the sanctuary?"

The leader glanced about curiously. A mocking smile flitted across the men's eyes. The warrior gripped the dagger by its hilt and tested its fearsome edge with his fingers.

Turning to Imaswan Wandarran, he asked, "Comrade, do you remember what I told you about points of articulation? Would you like me to show you how to find them?"

Leaning over the dagger's blade, he added coldly, "I told you that a man—like a sheep—has articulated joints and that you can't kill him if you don't understand them."

The leader gazed at him in astonishment. Then, staring at the men around him, he discovered that the coldness in their eyes was even more intense than that in his longtime comrade's.

Ahallum finished his statement, "This is the difference between heroism and courage. A man who knows the articulated joints earns the title of hero. Now that I've revealed my secret to you, I assume you're keen for me to corroborate it."

He turned coldly toward the leader and plunged the dagger into his chest with a blow faster than a flash of lightning. The blade sank into his chest up to the hilt. It sailed in with astonishing, even incredible, ease, as if the leader's chest were not a chest, as if it lacked a bony rib cage, a network of veins, or chunks of flesh, as if his chest were composed of teased wool, a cloud of steam, or . . . an air pocket. An air pocket is the only space that a foreign body could have penetrated with such ease. The leader emitted a groan of pain, but a restrained one.

The warrior shouted, "Here's your proof!"

The leader seized the hilt and said in a firm voice, as if he had not just been stabbed, "I thought you would never do that."

Ahallum replied frigidly, "We always see our error too late."

He did not give voice to his pain. He did not shake, and continued to hold the dagger that was planted in his chest. He replied, as if participating in a normal discussion in the council, "I admit I deserve this punishment because I, because I deceived myself and assumed that a true friend could be found in the desert."

He extracted the blade from his chest with the same astonishing ease—as if the blade had not been planted in a chest but thrust into a scabbard. He returned the dagger to the warrior. Ahallum stroked the edge of the blade with the palm of his hand and wiped the scant amount of blood off it. Then he presented the weapon to Imaswan Wandarran, who grabbed the hilt and brandished the blade in the air, saying, "Is it right for someone who thought himself more virtuous than anyone else to expect loyalty from his mates?"

The leader retorted firmly, "I've never claimed to be virtuous."

"You weren't satisfied with that but led everyone to imagine that you're the only one in whose heart the Spirit World resides."

"God forbid that someone like me should claim to possess the Spirit World."

"Had you not claimed to possess the Spirit World, you wouldn't have used the Law as a pretext for humiliating us. This is our response, because we are forced to defend ourselves."

He moved forward on his knees and stabbed the leader below his throat, but this was a different type of blow from the previous one. It made a sound, because the blade slammed into bones on its way in. The leader emitted a long cry of pain, like the groan of a dying man. He immediately withdrew the blade, however, and clung to the handle for a time before returning the dagger to Imaswan.

He said, "I knew that you were all hatching a conspiracy. But I didn't know man could surpass even the jinn in wickedness. Can gold turn men into jinn and change a comrade into an enemy in such a brief period?"

The chief merchant intervened, "You're further mistaken if you think we're taking revenge on you for confiscating our belongings or in order to acquire treasures of gold. You still don't grasp that the secret's in the game. You've never been good at playing games."

"The game?"

"You've forgotten that the whole affair, from the beginning, has merely been a game that's part of another game."

"I don't know what game you mean."

"Wasn't I a member of the group that visited your house and asked you to take power? Wasn't I a leader of the campaign that demanded a puppet leader who walks on two feet instead of a leader reposing in a mausoleum like a pile of bones? How can it have escaped you that all we wanted was a puppet? How can it have escaped you that this matter, like any other affair in the desert, was only a game? How, then, could you have grown arrogant and contentious, insisting on transforming the way of life in the valley?"

He held both hands against his chest. Blood had begun to flow and was soaking his shirt. In a voice that never registered any change, however, he said, "But I've never been good at games."

"Woe to any creature who isn't."

Ahallum repeated, with the intoxication of a person in an ecstatic trance, "Woe to any creature who doesn't excel at games nowadays."

Imaswan also repeated this phrase, followed by Amasis the Younger. They all repeated the phrase humbly, as if it were an ancient charm.

The chief merchant returned to the debate with the dying leader. "You say you've never been good at games but don't admit you didn't try to learn. You know a man can learn anything."

The wounded man shouted disapprovingly, "Even lying?"

The two-veiled man responded icily, "Lying is one of the pillars of life. Life isn't viable without lies. Do you know why?"

He did not wait for an answer. He said at once, "Because life is a lie!"

The leader gasped, "Life is a lie?"

The chief merchant did not reply to this question but made an even more extravagant claim, "For this reason, you should know that our holy Law is a game. We play games in everything we do. Even what we're doing now is a game."

The victim gasped out a feeble question. "According to your rules, stabbing a man is a game?"

"The real game isn't killing a man with the edge of a knife. The real game is to kill a man who doesn't play well with others."

The wounded man shook and struggled to comment, "I'm astonished to hear all this from the mouth of a man who once sang about commerce the way a passionate lover sings of his beautiful beloved."

"I'm afraid you got confused that day and misunderstood me. I've never denied that commerce is my true love. Similarly, today I don't deny that commerce is my favorite melody, my song I rely on to help me confront life's harshness. Playing games also necessarily involves songs. Commerce is my song, my consolation, my antidote, and the balm for my worries. So how can you expect me to refrain from singing my lyrics? How can you expect me not to repeat the melodies of my ecstasy?"

"I don't understood you today. I didn't understand you the other day. I've never understood you."

"I'm sad we part before you catch on."

He trembled again, feeling dizzy. He struggled to control himself and to regain mastery over a body weakened by loss of blood. He made an effort to recover the mellifluous expression of a nobleman. "At any rate, I can't help but thank all of you, because you . . . because you've spared me ever seeing your faces again."

The chief merchant resumed the debate zealously. "Your problem is that you've never been able to understand that a man has never acted as another man's friend—from day one—without also being his enemy. How can you aspire to happiness, if you don't care to understand this?"

"God forbid. . . ."

"Right: God forbid that a man should experience happiness if he hasn't learned how to play."

"Play your games, horse around, and know the happiness of living creatures, but reality belongs to the dead. Playing games is the lot of the living, but happiness is the secret of the dead."

"What do you mean by that?"

The wounded man did not reply. The chief merchant repeated his question, but the leader stubbornly refused to answer. The two-veiled man took the dagger from Imaswan and directed a ferocious blow to the body, which quivered. The chest emitted a groan. He withdrew the bloody dagger and presented it to Amasis the Younger, who advanced toward the body and brought the dagger down on the chest, which was washed in blood. He withdrew the bloody dagger but the painful moan from the chest did not end. It continued to emerge faintly, weakly, muffled, like a sleeper's snore.

The hero shouted, "Help me drag the body to the altar if you want to end this business at last."

They dragged the body to the corner altar. The warrior then took the dagger and sliced off the chain of amulets with the deftness of a hero. He tossed this necklace, which was composed of bits of leather, far away, and the man's breathing stopped at that same instant. Bringing the vicious blade down on the man's neck, he drew it across the throat with the same ferocity he would have used in slaughtering a sheep. After severing the head from the body, he told his peers, "You can carry the head out to the crowds in the plaza now."

Thun (The Swiss Alps)
The 24th of October to the 16th of November, 1997